My Own Worst Enemy

Emma L Smith

Published by Emma Smith at Createspace

My Own Worst Enemy

Front Matter

Thank you for purchasing my book. Keep up to date with my writing via my website:

www.emmalsmithbooks.co.uk

If you enjoy this book then please leave me a review. Your words are the greatest gift you can give.

My beautiful cover was designed by Anne Notghi

My Own Worst Enemy

Dedication

Daddy,

Miss you xx

To Helen @ All Booked Out

Check the acknowledgements!

Emma L Smith xx

My Own Worst Enemy

Prologue - Ben

I sat side by side with Trick on cheap plastic chairs while we waited for the doctor to examine her. His hands shook and his face was pale. The hospital stench was clogging up my throat and making it near impossible to gather a full breath.

"I can't lose her Ben. I just can't. There has to be a way to fix this." He sounded as desperate as I felt. I had no idea what the solution was but I knew the whole thing was a complete mess.

I'd already seen enough death and pain in my life and now I had to sit here, completely helpless and unable to do anything but wait. "We'll find a way Trick. Maybe she just needs time." My sigh was heavy and laced with the feeling of inevitability. Whatever the outcome, none of us would feel any better.

Trick grunted. "This is my fault. I should have seen the signs sooner. Annie…" Tears pooled in his eyes as he choked on his words and I wished I had a way to relieve his pain even for a moment.

"Don't blame yourself. Everything happens for a reason right?" I wondered how many more clichés I could pull out of my locker before I ran dry.

Trick stood suddenly, his body poised for action. "Fuck that. I can fix this. I don't care what they say, I'm going in there."

I was up and blocking his path before he could move forward. "Trick, no. Give them time to examine her first. Let's wait and see what they say, okay?" Trying to control my tone to sound calm and relaxed was near impossible as it was so far from how I actually felt.

He nodded but his gaze was still firmly fixed on the door to her hospital room. My hands rested on his shoulders and I willed him to sit back down. I focused solely on the erratic thump of my heartbeat as we faced off, every muscle in my frame aching to run into that room with him. Excruciatingly slowly, he eased back down.

We had three minutes of calm before he was up and pacing the hallway like a caged panther. "What's taking so long? They should be finished by now."

"Just let them work Trick. Why don't we get a drink or something from the canteen?" And the award for the most pointless suggestion of the day goes to…

He shook his head. "I don't want to leave her. She might need me." His eyes flicked back to the door and I slumped back into the plastic chair knowing that there would be nothing I could say to calm him down. The woman he loved was in there and his natural instinct was always going to be to go to her. Judging by the frantic look he was carrying and the pent up energy burning through him, it would take a bulldozer to keep him out of that room.

Two men approached us with stern looks, dressed like crashers at a wedding. They were both shorter and older and had the air of people who were weighing up their options before a fight breaks out in a bar. Together Trick and I were tall and muscular and to strangers, certainly intimidating. There was no question as to who would win if it came down to it. They stopped in front of us and waited for Trick to look up.

The sadness was gone in an instant and his steely gaze swept them over, coming to the same conclusion I had. No matter who these men were, they were looking for trouble. "Can I help you?" He rose to his feet and towered over the men making his intentions clear. He would not back down and was prepared to fight it out.

One of the men swallowed heavily, clearly nervous. "Trick Travers?"

He sized them up with a squint before nodding. "Yeah that's me. What the fuck do you want?"

The other man reached into his pocket and my body instinctively braced. "You're under arrest for murder. You have the right to remain silent…."

His voice trailed off inside my head as my brain fogged. Trick didn't resist in the slightest and he sagged with the knowledge of a situation too far beyond his control.

Chapter One

"Fuck him B. If he can't see what an amazing girl you are then fuck him. Come out with me tonight. Please?" My brother's pleading brown eyes glared down at me and I knew I wouldn't be able to refuse him when he gave me that look. Over the years, my favourite toys, pocket money and countless cover stories to our mum had all been garnered from me with just that look.

I rolled my eyes. "Let me get dressed then." I slumped in defeat as he sparkled in triumph.

My twin brother Ben was tall and lithe with a face that melted girl's hearts everywhere he went. He had a million dollar smile that had panties dropping as he walked past with a confident swagger that told the world that not only was he fully aware of how he looked but that he was also not in the slightest bit interested. Many a woman had tried and spectacularly failed to win his attention as he stared blankly through them, oblivious, his mind elsewhere. He once told me that he could never feel anything for a woman unless she captured his mind first and had never found anyone that he could bear to hold more than a two minute conversation with. Ben went out of his way to dissuade them, covering his body in tattoos and dressing like he had just rolled out of bed at all times. He never made an effort, ever, but somehow it only made him more desirable to the gaggle of giggly girls he had to fight his way through to get anywhere. We'd never spoken about his sex life but it wouldn't surprise me either way if his number was in triple digits or zero. He was always hard to read and secretive, his mind often racing a million miles an hour. The one thing he had never failed to do was love me. Whenever I needed him, he was there. No explanation required, he would drop everything and be at my side. I loved him for that and so never once slipped him one of my friend's numbers when they begged me to or pushed him to justify himself and force him into a relationship he didn't want.

While my brother had been stealing all the good genes in the womb, I had been left with the scraps. I was a whole foot shorter than Ben and while he carried a lean muscular figure that seemingly required no maintenance and allowed him to eat absolutely anything he wanted, I couldn't even walk past a McDonald's without putting on weight. I knew I wasn't fat but I was definitely on the heavier side of what would be considered curvy and it was a constant struggle to keep it under control. While my brother got the thick lustrous hair from our dad, I got lumbered with the fine thin hair of our nanna. He got the strong cheekbones and perfect jaw and I got the round undefined features that made us look completely unrelated. In fact while women were fawning all over my brother, I often had to produce my driving licence so they would believe we even came from the same family. It shouldn't have bothered me but it did. Sometimes I really despised my gene thief of a twin.

My Own Worst Enemy

While Ben sailed through his last twenty eight years without any sort of relationship under his belt, I was incapable of not being in one. Since I'd been fourteen I had gone from guy to guy like a girl who just didn't know how to be alone. I'd never spent more than a week single and every relationship I had ever had ended in disaster. Some stuck around for longer than others but not one of them could understand why I didn't feel so grateful to be with them that I didn't sleep with them. Strictly speaking, it wasn't a conscious decision, but deep down in the pit of my stomach, buried far away from my active grey matter, I knew there was only ever going to be one guy I would ever want to have sex with. As I knew it wasn't going to happen, ever, I unsuccessfully drifted around trying to find my place in the world.

Trick Travers was Ben's best friend and they had known each other since they were eleven. His father had been some kind of street magician and had thought the name Trick was hilarious. I thought it made him sound like a movie star and from the moment he first walked through my front door, I had been head over heels in love with him. The problem was that while Trick was the only guy for me, there had only been one girl for him and it wasn't me. Annie Armstrong had captured his heart like he had mine and he loved her with a forceful passion that made mountains move. She was his whole world and when she was around, it was like he could see nothing else. Everyone had thought they would get married and have hundreds of beautiful babies. Except the fates were not aligned that way and four years ago she had died. They had been out for dinner for their anniversary when she collapsed and died in his arms from an aneurism. Trick had taken it really hard and I barely saw him anymore. When I did, he was a shadow of his former self, like a part of him had died right along with her.

Ben had been Trick's constant companion ever since, making sure he wasn't alone. As he started to get back on his feet, Ben had never pushed Trick to go out or do anything he didn't want to and I had purposefully kept my distance. Every time I looked into his deep grey eyes, my heart broke for everything he'd lost and I couldn't contain it. The last thing he needed was my sympathy so I stayed away. Ben had told me that the last few months had been easier and Trick was really starting to deal with it better now, even going out with the guys a few times. I wasn't sure how much of it was a fake plastic smile he had pasted on to stop everyone feeling sorry for him but I hoped it was the road to recovery.

As I applied my lip gloss, I thought about Andy who I had just broken it off with after I went to surprise him with a muffin and found him saying goodbye to a girl on the doorstep, with his tongue. The feelings he had for me would never have reached the epic heights that Trick's had for Annie and I was determined that if I couldn't have that then I wouldn't have anything. Nothing less than heart stopping, all out, knee trembling declarations of love would do and without them, I wouldn't even let them near my knickers.

When I heard the voice of Ben's friend Jay downstairs, I knew tonight would be a long one. When my brother was out with his friends, it was all about the booze. They never went out to dance or pick up girls and despite the excessive amounts of alcohol they consumed, they very rarely got in fights either. I always enjoyed hanging out with them because they never had any agenda other than having a good time together. Weirdly, my list of exes had never felt comfortable around them and after mumbling through a few awkward conversations had always left early. In fact, on a few occasions they had even left before they'd finished their first drink. I always had fun with them though and they made it easy to forget anything that was going on around me and just be.

My brother was a part owner of a tattoo shop and Jay worked for him. They never had anything other than a casual easy going friendship and I doubted Ben ever felt the need to manage him. Jay was all out tattoos and piercings and would always have something new to show off. Once he ran out of space on his body, he decided to shave his head and do his skull too. Anyone who didn't know him would definitely take a step back but he was the sweetest and softest guy I'd ever met, eternally armed with a smile and a compliment.

Ben's circle was completed by Rob and Ray who had been the only other set of twins in our year at school. Unlike Ben and I, they were completely identical and I loved them both. We had all grown up together and I had watched them develop from scrawny teenagers to handsome and intelligent young men. They were both downright outrageous where women were concerned and there were many legendary tales of them sleeping with the same girl or running scams on them until the poor girls didn't know what was going on. They had never once failed to make me smile and I figured that if the girls were stupid enough to go along with it then they only had themselves to blame.

I pulled my hair up into a messy ponytail, padding down the stairs in my jeans and converse. I couldn't help but run my hand through the trimmed mohawk Jay was sporting that he'd inexplicably sprayed dark green. He turned and smiled widely at me. "Hey Beth, how's things?"

Jay's eyes roamed my stomach where my top lifted slightly showing a touch of flesh around my waistband. I smacked him on the arm. "Good thanks perv. How's you?"

He nodded his state of well-being with a cheeky grin for being caught ogling me and followed me into the kitchen where Ben had already laid out three shots. "I heard you broke up with Andy Pandy. Good riddance I say, that guy was a fucking douche."

I lifted the glass to my lips and slicked the shot down my throat, banging it heavily against the counter. "Amen to that brother." He gave me a very manly fist bump as I held out his shot glass for him to accept.

McKinley's was only at the bottom of our road and as such had become our drinking place of choice. We sometimes made grand schemes to go into town and see the bright lights but they never came to fruition. If any of the guys couldn't make it home, we had plenty of room and it wasn't uncommon to see one of them stretched out on the sofa of a morning. It had once been a working men's club back in the seventies and then a wine bar but now the current owner Nate had turned it into a proper pub with live music most weekends. Nate's daughter Leanne had been trying to get Ben to notice her since we first stepped over the threshold on our eighteenth birthday. Despite her outrageously shameless flirting, we liked it and were there most weeks either with the guys or just the two of us. Over the years we'd managed to get to know all the regulars and they happily tolerated our playful drunkenness.

As the three of us walked in, Leanne noticed immediately and stood a little straighter, pushing her breasts out. Ben ordered drinks as a thick muscular arm wrapped round my waist. The owner of the arm's head bent low to my ear and whispered. "So I hear you're single again. Any chance I can get you out of those jeans now?" I turned and threw my arms around Ray with a smile.

"Cheeky fucker. How are you?"

He pushed me out so he could look at me. "All the better for seeing you sweetheart. Do I need to go and break that fucker's legs or what?"

I knew he was only half joking so I shook my head quickly. "No, he's not worth it. Although if I change my mind, you'll be the first one I'll call." Rob and Ray had taken it upon themselves to look after me and had often been the ones who arrived in doorways to collect my things on numerous occasions, kind of like burglars with keys. Despite their good looks, when they stood together they were as wide as they were tall and would never back down. I always felt safe around them and they had never failed to come through for me.

"Bethany Lewis! As I live and breathe! Get your fine ass over here and give me a hug!" My skin tingled at the sound of Trick's deep rugged voice and I instantly span round to face him, throwing myself into his waiting arms. He pulled me in for a tight squeeze, his hands wrapping easily around my body and I sighed as I sank into him. It had been at least eight months since I'd last seen him and I didn't want to let go. Being encased against his body felt like coming home.

Trick seemed to feel the same way as it was only my brother handing him a drink that made him look up and pull away. He kept one arm draped over my shoulder casually and I held onto his fingers with mine. Their bottles chinked together in greeting as we walked over to our usual table. Everyone was pleased to see Trick and greeted him warmly but not once did he remove his body from mine. As the guys talked, I couldn't help but let my mind wander and think about the first time I'd ever met him.

I stepped out of the shower and reached for a towel but Ben had been in before me and the only towel left hanging on the rail was practically a napkin. At fourteen, I had become acutely aware of my body and freaked out if anyone came close to seeing the slightest patch of bare skin. I levered the door open cautiously and stuck my head out. "Ben!" I screamed down the hallway for him but I could hear music coming loudly from his room.

After the fifth scream, his head poked out from his room. "What?" Clearly he was angry I had disturbed him.

My eyes widened in annoyance. "Where are all the fucking towels?"

He grinned at me and stepped across the hall to the airing cupboard. He sauntered over to me and handed me a towel like he was doing me a huge favour. I snatched it out of his hand. "You have no manners. Who takes the last towel and doesn't replace it?"

He laughed at me, long and hard, right in my face. My fists balled tightly with a desire to punch him on the nose. "Relax, it wasn't even me. Do I look like I've had a shower?"

I glared at him as he swept his hands over his body to display his lack of dampness. "Well who was it then, the bloody toothfairy?"

He shook his head at me and walked away. "Maybe, who knows?"

I grunted in disapproval and slammed the bathroom door. As I unfolded the towel I realised this one was not much bigger. I managed to just wrap it around me to cover up the most essential parts but that was about it. Keeping my fingers tight to the seam, I pulled the door open violently in bid to rush to my room before anyone saw me.

I walked straight into an object, instinctively screamed and then released my grip on the towel. I looked upwards and realised the thing I'd walked into was a person. Not just a person. The most beautiful person I'd ever seen. Cloudy grey eyes filled his amazing face. His jaw was strong and solid and his hair was thick and messy. His body was humming with strength and I felt mine groan for his. A tiny smile twitched at the corner of his perfectly kissable lips and I realised I was staring and naked. I screamed again and ran back behind the door, slamming it in his face.

"Hi." He spoke the word from the other side of the door and even through the steam, I could see in the mirror that my face was bright red. I leaned back against the door and hoped that he'd leave and never come back. "Are you planning on coming out anytime soon?" I heard him snigger and I scrunched my face up in embarrassment.

"Errr, not really planning on it." God I was such a dork. How the hell was I going to get out of this?

"You err... left your towel out here." I smacked my head against the door and took a deep breath. Okay, I can do this. Just open the door and act like nothing happened. I pulled the door open a crack and grabbed the towel from his hand. Wrapping it around myself, I attempted a casual nonchalant walk back to my room. "I'm Trick by the way."

I turned to face him, his smirk making me feel beyond embarrassed and into a new realm of needing to bury my face in the sand. "Oh." It was all I could manage. I'd heard Ben talk about him and I knew they were friends but as we weren't due to go to the same school until next year, I'd not even been able to ogle him in class. I just wanted to run away and get some distance between us so I carried on walking and closed my bedroom door behind me.

I slipped my robe on once inside, already feeling better now I was more covered but when I turned around, he was standing in my doorway, leaning casually against the frame. I really hoped he had only just arrived and not been there when I replaced the towel with my robe. "Is that all I get? 'Oh'." He smirked again cheekily and my mouth opened and closed a few times. He came in and sat down on my bed, seemingly unconcerned about the lack of an invitation.

"Err, what are you doing?" I couldn't believe how rude he was. Or how utterly gorgeous. Part of me wanted

to throw him out and part of me wanted to drop the towel and throw myself at him. Teenage hormones were an absolute bitch.

The smirk broadened and his eyes were alight with mischief. "I thought I'd come and talk to you Tink."

I frowned. "That's not my name." I folded my arms, annoyed with him, my face heating to epic proportions.

He shrugged. "Sure it is. So what sort of music do you like?" Leaning back nonchalantly, he seemed like he had all the time in the world and one single focus. Me.

I blinked rapidly, unable to work out what was happening. Ben's frame appeared in my doorway. "Come on man, we've still got loads to do."

Trick nodded to him and stood up. "See you later Tink." He winked at me and walked away as I ran to the door, slamming it sharply behind him. God he was so rude and obnoxious but wow, he was hot.

Trick's voice pulled me out of my daydream and back to the present. "I hear the band tonight are off the chain. You've seen them right Jay?" Trick gestured towards Jay with his eyes.

Jay nodded. "Yeah man, they're sick. You been working?"

Trick shrugged. "Yeah a little. Just came back from three months with some fucking little pop princess. Made my friggin' ears bleed but it pays the bills." He tilted his bottle nonchalantly. Trick was a session musician and there wasn't an instrument you could put in front of him that he couldn't play. He was often going on tours or recording with acts because they needed someone to play with them. The solitary and nomadic nature of his job was a perfect fit for him. He could come and go as he pleased without having to answer to anyone or get too involved.

As they continued their assault of the artist Trick had worked with, I considered him carefully. It was almost as if the last four years hadn't happened. His cheeky grin was plastered across his face and his eyes danced with merriment and mischief. His arm wrapped across my shoulder was testament to the fact that he'd been working out and as he pulled me closer, I nestled against him and felt the pure muscle with a sigh of contentment. He was no longer the man that had refused to eat and had let his grief consume him. I looked up at him with a smile, barely able to contain the relief and joy I felt at having him relatively back to normal. It was more than an outward façade, it was genuine progress.

Trick caught me staring at him and looked down with a grin. "What you grinning at?" He eyed me suspiciously like I was making fun of him somehow.

I shrugged. "Nothing, just happy that's all." He pulled me even closer to him and my leg slipped over his thigh. He grabbed it firmly with his free hand and held me securely in place.

"I thought you were nursing a broken heart." His thumb rubbed the underside of my knee and I felt a pleasant tingle all the way up to between my legs.

I grimaced, all too aware that my relationship melt down was nothing in comparison to the pain trick was carrying around. “No, not for that wanker.” I hadn’t realised until I’d said it, but the words rang true to me then. I did have a broken heart but it was Trick that had done the breaking.

He looked sad for a moment and when he spoke his voice was barely a whisper. “I can’t imagine any guy that gets to hold you in his arms ever wanting to let you go Tink." His features hardened and he suddenly became much more serious and a touch terrifying. "Do I need to hurt this cunt or what?”

I bristled a little at hearing the C word. My brother used it so rarely and I couldn’t recall a time I had ever said it. Something about it felt awfully vicious and raw. I couldn’t be mad at him though because he’d called me Tink. He’d always used it as my nickname although I had no idea why. It felt good to hear it again, familiar and comforting. “No, it’s fine. I should have known better.”

Trick sucked on his top lip for a moment as he searched my face. “Don’t ever do that. Don’t put this on yourself, you deserve better. Much fucking better. No-one gets to do that to you, ever.” His grip on my leg tightened and I felt the intensity behind what he said.

I turned my head away, blinking back a tear. My voice came out all pained and shaky. “I… it was my fault… I should have….” I choked back a sob, unable to go any further. I knew exactly what the problem was. If I'd have slept with Andy then he never would have cheated. Even the thought of being with a man that wasn't Trick just made me long for the things I'd never have. It was so overwhelming and impossible to verbalise to Trick. He'd never understand my infatuation with him and the last thing I wanted was for him to purposely keep his distance.

Trick slipped his fingers under my chin and forced me to look at him. His eyes burned with a fire I’d not seen in them in a long time. “No Tink. You didn’t have to do anything.” I sniffed and felt tears falling heavily down my cheeks now. Trick closed his eyes for a moment and then pulled me fully onto his lap letting me cry into his shoulder. As the sense of pathetic desperation over took me, I let him comfort me and he didn't pull away, holding me tightly and stroking my back gently. When Rob got up to go the bar, Trick's hand left me for a moment to tap him. Rob turned and lowered his face to the other side of mine. Trick whispered but I heard every word. "Find out where he lives, I'm going to kill this prick."

I wanted to be able to say something to him, anything to prevent what he'd threatened but all I could do was cry and let him hold me. Eventually I got to a state that allowed me to breathe a little easier and tears weren't pouring out of my eyes at every opportunity. As I reluctantly eased out of our embrace, Trick smoothed my hair back and rubbed my cheeks softly with his thumb. "You want me to take you home Tink?" I nodded in between sniffs. He looked at me for a moment, checking that I wasn't going to burst into tears again. "I just gotta talk to Ben for a sec. Stay here with Jay, okay?" I nodded again and Jay put his arm around me warmly, allowing me to lay my head on his shoulder. It didn't feel as good as it had with Trick but it was definitely comforting.

Trick tapped my brother on the shoulder and gestured to the other side of the room. I watched as they made their way over to a corner. Trick held his arms out wide as he spoke, Ben's eyes narrowing and then flicking to me. Without warning, Ben punched Trick right in the face. Trick's head rocked back slightly but he didn't retaliate. Jay stroked my back and I realised I'd let out a little scream when the punch landed. Ray and Rob hadn't moved from the table either and I wondered if they knew what was going on. Ben was in full attack stance now, his shoulders tight and his fists balled. Trick rubbed his face where the blow had struck but went right back to holding his arms out wide in a gesture of peace. I couldn't see his face but his head was definitely shaking. Ben's eyes kept darting back to me, wide with horror. I turned to Jay, demanding an explanation. “What is going on?” Jay shrugged. “Fucking tell me now or I’m going over there to find out.” I pointed to the source as if Jay wouldn't know what I was referring to.

Making a move to lift myself from the chair, Jay pushed me back. “Alright, keep your panties on. Trick’s just asking something, that’s all.” He seemed oddly calm and infuriatingly knowledgeable.

My eyes shot back over to them and Trick was still talking, my brother clearly not keen to listen. “What? What’s he asking?” I was irritated now. All I wanted to do was go home and lie down but this just seemed so epic. My brother and Trick had the most solid friendship in the world. Or at least I always thought so.

Jay shook his head. “Don’t worry about it.” I rolled my eyes and tried to stand up again. Jay moved himself so that he could physically hold me down. “B, please? Just let them work it out. I promise you, everything will be fine. None of us will let them get hurt.” He swirled his finger around gesturing to the twins who both nodded earnestly.

I sat back in my seat defiantly, crossing my arms in frustration. The look of anger and hatred washing across Ben's face was really scaring me. He grabbed Trick by the throat and body slammed him against the wall. Trick again made no move to throw him off even though I'd seen him flip my brother off a million times in play fights. My stomach clenched with anxiety but still the boys sat stoically silent, watching the action. I knew what Jay had said was true, they wouldn't let it get out of control but it didn't prevent the ball of worry building inside me. It seemed like a lifetime before Ben finally let go, holding out his fist to Trick who enthusiastically punched it. They returned with arms around each other, smiling, only Trick's bloody cheek as evidence that anything had passed between them.

Trick took his seat next to me and I instantly began fussing over him, checking that he was okay. He smiled at me but his eyes were on Ben. "I'm alright, don't worry. Still want to go?" I nodded. "Come on then, let's go." He held out his hand for me as he stood and I accepted it, shooting a quick glance at Ben who looked as if he was about to smash his beer glass against the table.

"See you at home?" I sent him a confused smile and he stared at me murderously before allowing himself a single nod of the head. We said our goodbyes and I noticed there was something almost gleeful in the way the boys bid Trick farewell while Ben stayed gloomy and dark as Trick waved at him, barely looking up from the table.

As soon as we were outside I stepped in front of Trick and took his wrists in my hands. They were so thick that I could barely get purchase on him but I persisted anyway. "Okay, what the fuck was that?"

He shook his head and effortlessly dropped my hands, swinging his arm over my shoulder. "Don't worry about it. Guy stuff." He started walking, dragging me along with him.

I wrestled myself out from underneath him, slamming my palm into his chest with all my might. He didn't even flinch. "Trick! Just tell me. I've never seen Ben look like that, I'm worried about him." I looked down in an attempt to pull the girl card and guilt him in to telling me.

He slid his arms around me and pulled me in tightly for a hug. "I just had to ask him something but he said yes in the end so don't worry about it. Please Tink?" I tipped my head upwards so I could look into his eyes. They displayed a mixture of fear and remorse and I knew that whatever he'd asked had been a big deal for him. As soon as I nodded my agreement, he grinned brightly. "Come on then, let's get you tucked up in bed."

He held my hand tightly all the way back to my house and didn't let go until we were in my room. While I got changed in the bathroom he perched himself on the edge of my bed and when I came back in his head was in his hands. I stepped cautiously towards him, pushing his knees apart so I was between his legs and brushed his hair out of his face. He looked up at me with pure sadness. “What’s wrong?”

He swallowed hard and frowned. “Are you working tomorrow?” There was an edge of uncertainty in his tone.

I shook my head, confused that my shift pattern was causing him such distress. “What’s going on Trick? Please tell me, I’m worried about you.”

His hands lifted to my waist and his thumbs caressed me softly. His head dropped so it was leaning against my stomach and all I could do was stroke it and shush him soothingly. We stood like that for a long time until I thought that my knees were going to cramp up. Without any warning he suddenly pushed me gently away from him and stood up, moving to my doorway. He stopped, his had resting on the woodwork but his back to me. “Tink…. I…. FUCK!” He exclaimed and slammed his fist solidly against my doorframe making me yelp and jump back slightly. He shook his head vigorously. “I’ve gotta go.” Without another word or turning in my direction, he sprinted down the stairs and slammed the front door shut behind him.

Chapter Two

Over the next few days I tried everything I could to get the truth out of my brother but he was much better at keeping things from me than I was at getting them out of him. I tried shouting, begging, crying, everything, but he was like an immovable object. I had called and text Trick too but got no response either. Finally after a particularly difficult shift at work where every single customer was a complete arsehole I decided to go and hear it directly from the horse's mouth. I practically stomped round to Trick's front door building up a demanding fury inside myself.

We hadn't finished clearing up at the bar until after three and by the time I got to Trick's it was easily four in the morning. The house was in complete darkness but I pounded angrily on the door anyway, refusing to give in until he answered. I hammered for a good few minutes, my hands going numb with the force until a light came on in the hallway and I heard him chuntering from behind the door. He flung it open with genuine force, a growl on his features. As soon as he caught sight of me, his fierceness dropped away into sadness and regret and I could see him debating whether or not to close the door in my face. “What do you want Tink?” He seemed defeated, like he'd already fought the war and lost.

His face was covered in stubble and he reeked of alcohol and sex. His boxers and a tight grey t-shirt were the only things covering up his magnificent body. I shoved my foot in the doorway so he couldn’t close it on me. “I want to know what the fuck is going on Trick. You freak out in my room and won’t talk to me and Ben’s walking around like someone killed his fucking dog. Just tell me the truth. Please?” My anger was starting to fade as I stared at his helpless and remorseful features.

He opened his mouth to speak and then glanced back to the stairwell. “Now’s not a good time Tink.” He grimaced and I just knew he had a woman in his bed. A sob threatened to choke me to death as I struggled to breathe. I don’t know why the idea of him sleeping with someone destroyed me so much but I felt betrayed somehow. He'd never been mine but I wanted him to be, more than anything.

The sound of my palm striking his cheek echoed out across the moonlit road. I gasped in shock at what I’d done and instantly crumpled into a distraught crying mess on his doorstep feeling hurt and betrayed and a million other things I had no right to feel. He kneeled down to my side and dragged me into an embrace, rubbing my back gently as my howls of pain and frustration bounced around the alcove. I was vaguely aware of him lifting me and placing me softly on the sofa. It was only when the physical contact was withdrawn that the full trauma of what I’d just done really hit me and I clutched a throw pillow, sinking my head into it in shame and humiliation.

“Yeah just come and get her, she needs you.” I was aware of Trick speaking and I knew he’d called Ben. The knowledge only compounded my emotions all I could focus on was how ridiculous I was being. If I ever truly thought that I had a chance with Trick then my behaviour was doing absolutely nothing to help that along. Yet I couldn't find any other way to be. My emotional state was too raw and unfiltered. I had absolutely no control over myself and that was terrifying.

I heard a girl’s voice call Trick's name right before my brother came barrelling through the door. He looked from me to Trick to the girl and then threw himself at Trick with such force that they both slammed into the carpet. “What the fuck did you do? I fucking warned you!” Ben got the upper hand quickly and straddled Trick, punching him hard in the face. I wasn’t sure if it was me or the girl who screamed but the sound lingered almost as long as the crack of Trick's cheekbone snapping.

Trick flipped my brother off him and stood. "I didn't fucking touch her! Tell him Tink. Tell him I didn't do this to you." His eyes swung towards me, pleading with me to speak in his defence.

My brother paused for a moment as I looked between Trick and the girl who I realised was completely topless and only wearing the world's tiniest thong. The thought of his hands all over her made me feel sick and all I could do was look at my brother as my lip trembled and a small whimper escaped me.

Ben rounded back on Trick. "I'm going to fucking kill you!" Trick tried to put his hands out to speak but Ben wasn't ready to hear it. He threw Trick forcibly against the wall and landed a punch in his gut. Trick slid down the wall with a groan and suddenly I realised that I had to do something before Ben killed him.

"Ben wait, stop." My voice was barely audible but he heard it and turned.

Ben came round to my side and lowered himself so he could look me over properly. “What happened Beth? Tell me what happened please? Did he hurt you?” His eyes flashed with anger and then he was back to cooing softly around me, running his hands over me to check for damage.

I shook my head. “It wasn’t Trick, I just… I thought…. I…. it’s not his fault Ben, please?” I couldn’t verbalise the inner turmoil within me. It was pent up jealousy and frustration over seeing Trick with another girl and my own disappointment at my inability to take what I wanted. If Trick was dating again then I wanted to be the one he was dating.

Trick groaned as he stood up shakily. “I tried to tell you man. I would never hurt her.” I grimaced at his words knowing that he had unknowingly hurt me tonight, just not physically. Ben’s eyes lifted to Trick but came swiftly back to me.

“Beth? Did he hurt you? Just tell me.” He moved his head so I couldn’t escape his stare. I closed my eyes and swallowed, not wanting Ben to hurt Trick but also not wanting to lie to my brother.

"He didn't touch me." It came out as a garbled mumble but Ben bit his lip and nodded in understanding.

He stood up and held out his hand for me. As we reached to door he turned and pointed to Trick. "Stay away from my fucking sister. If I catch you within a mile of her I'm gonna rip your fucking dick off. Are we clear?"

Trick looked between me and my brother for a long time before answering, seemingly making a decision. "No can do man." The words were barely out of his mouth when Ben let go of my hand and stormed towards Trick.

They were in each other's faces now, foreheads pressed together like duelling stags. "What the fuck did you say?" Ben tried to push Trick in the chest but this time Trick wasn't going to roll over so easily and stood firm against the pressure.

"You heard me. It's not gonna happen. I'll see her again, end of." Trick said it almost with a chuckle, taunting my brother. I was utterly confused as to why he was fighting this so hard, anyone else would have backed down before now. Particularly as he was clearly involved with the tramp in the thong. She was probably a really lovely girl but right at this moment, I hated her almost as much as I hated myself.

Ben's fists clenched tightly and he swung out towards Trick but Trick ducked and then pushed Ben's waist making him stumble backwards. "I don't want to fight you man but I will. For her, I will. Now stop this crazy shit and take her home before one of us does something we regret." He swiped at his cheek with the back of his hand, blood dripping off onto the carpet. In a strange moment of disconnection I couldn't help wondering how difficult it was to get blood out of fabric.

Ben swayed slightly and put one hand against the wall, searching Trick's eyes. "Cocks out?"

Trick nodded slowly with a grin. "Cocks out, all the fucking way man. I promise you." He fisted his heart in a primal, masculine gesture.

Ben didn't take his eyes off Trick as he spoke. "Beth. Go get in the car." I started to protest but he shut me down. "Now Beth."

I stomped down the path more confused now than I had been when I arrived, feeling lost and helpless. I saw the girl from Trick's house making a hasty stilletoed exit across the lawn before Ben came out and threw himself into his seat, starting the engine and pulling away without a word. I tried to speak to him but he cut me off, turning up the stereo so loud it made my eardrums hurt.

Jay came over the next morning to pick Ben up for work as he'd insisted I take the car so I could drive back from work. I ran down the stairs to greet him hoping to get the chance to speak to him before Ben came down. He greeted me with a warm hug and a smile.

"Can I ask you something?" I whispered conspiratorially as we made our way into the kitchen.

"Anything B you know that." He grabbed a mug and put coffee and hot water into it as he spoke.

"What does 'cocks out' mean?" It was the one thing above everything else that was mystifying me the most about last night.

He sniggered. "It's the song innit?" I frowned and shook my head, not understanding what he meant. He raised an eyebrow at my complete naivety. "You know? When Ben and Trick were in that band?" I shrugged and he began to sing the line that suddenly felt terribly familiar. "Cocks out....for true love."

I blinked rapidly taking in what he'd just said and trying to make sense of it all in my head as Ben came down stairs and stood behind me. I turned and frowned at him, his body instantly tense and alert. "What?" He practically spat at me, frustration bubbling to the surface of his normally relaxed features.

In our whole lives, Ben had always been there for me, no matter what and now I felt like he was slipping away from me. I was looking at a stranger standing in my kitchen and it made me feel uneasy and desolate. I lifted my hand to his arm, wanting to feel the comfort of his skin. "Ben…"

He flinched slightly at first but then exhaled, some of the tension draining from his frame. "Beth. Shit. I'm sorry. Come here." He threw his arms around me and held me tightly, kissing the top of my head. "I'm just trying to look out for you, you know that right?" I nodded knowing that there was nothing Ben could ever do that would change the fact I loved him, he always had my best interests at heart in every action he ever took. "I'll call you later okay?" I nodded and watched him go with a small wave to Jay.

My mind raced through all the things that had happened and I just couldn't put all the pieces together properly. It was like some kind of infuriating impossipuzzle and I couldn't see the lines because of all the fucking baked beans. I flicked the shower on and let the scolding water sear across my skin, hoping that the answer would miraculously come to me but it didn't.

Thoroughly confused and annoyed, I decided just to go in to work early so at least I'd have something to take my mind off the chaos that was my life. As soon as I walked through the door I knew it had been a bad idea. Andy's figure was completely recognisable to me even from behind as he sat at the bar nursing a pint. I rolled my eyes and slipped out back to put my bag away.

I came out behind the bar and moved closer to him, gasping as he looked into my eyes. White tape criss-crossed his clearly broken nose and two black eyes disguised his normally crystal clear irises. He tilted his chin in greeting.

"Andy? What happened to you?" He looked a complete mess and I couldn't help but feel some sympathy for him.

He snorted and winced, clearly in pain. "What do you think happened Beth?" He gestured to his face as if I was a complete idiot and hadn't noticed his bruises. "Look, I just came to apologise to you. I was a dick and I'm sorry. Can you forgive me?" He swallowed and pleaded with me with his eyes.

I frowned recognising that this wasn't Andy talking. "Why would you say that?"

His lips pursed tightly and I could see him waging a battle with himself. "Because it's the truth. Please accept my apology."

There was something wrong, Andy never apologised for anything and I could see that he didn't mean the words either. I shook my head with another frown. "No, I don't accept it. I don't believe you."

He sneered now and his hand thumped heavily against the bar, the real Andy leaping to the surface. "Fine, don't accept it. Y'know what? I'm not fucking sorry. If you weren't such a prick teasing little bitch then I wouldn't have had to go elsewhere. Tell your friends to back the fuck off." He hissed the words at me before pushing off from his chair and storming out, leaving the two way door swinging wildly on its hinges.

I felt like I'd been thumped in the chest and had to hold my hand tightly to my breast to try and regain control over my breathing. Lena who worked the afternoon shift saw what was happening and came rushing to my side, shunting me into a chair and bringing me a glass of water.

"You okay Beth? Can I call someone for you?" I shook my head not wanting to disrupt the tenuous peace between me and Ben.

I gulped down the water as if I'd been in the desert for a hundred years. It took nearly an hour but I finally got myself under control and went back to work. Lena slipped me a few concerned glances but she didn't bring it up and as it got busier I found my mind starting to calm under a sea of orders. By the time Dan came in for his shift I was back to normal and we laughed and joked our way through the first few hours, occasionally spraying each other with water and dropping slices of lemon down each other's backs.

I went out to collect glasses when the bar seemed to quiet down a little and as I shoved my way through throngs of bodies clustered together a hand reached out and grabbed my ass. I spun round and saw a cocky little shit grinning madly at me. “What the fuck dude? Seriously?” I held my hands up to show that he was being a prick.

He stood up and licked his lips. “Come on baby, let me take you home tonight and see what you taste like.”

My face visibly contorted at his words as the grossness of them filtered through. “Jesus, no fucking way man.” Working in a bar always brought its fair share of guys who felt that they had some rights to my body. I was used to it and could stand up for myself but it didn't stop it being creepy.

I took a step back and he reached out to grab me again. Before he could make contact, a hand shot out of nowhere and twisted his arm behind his back. “She said no dickhead. Now back the fuck off before I put your face through that wall."

My mouth fell open at the sight of Trick and the guy held his other hand up in submission. Trick twisted tighter and I saw the guy grimace. "Now apologise to the nice lady and run along home."

The guy looked at me with pure fear in his eyes and I knew he was hurting badly. "Sss.s..sorry." Trick released him and he scrambled for the door as if his life depended on it.

Trick grinned at me with a cocky half smile. My face was thunderous as I looked at him and the grin slid from his lips quickly. "It was you wasn't it? You smashed Andy's face up?"

Trick breathed in awkwardly and I knew it was him beyond all shadow of a doubt. He tried an apologetic smile as he rubbed his neck. "Don't be mad Tink, the dickhead deserved it."

I rolled my eyes and sighed, twisting away from him. He reached out and grabbed my wrist lightly making me stop and turn back. “Just don’t Trick. I can’t handle this shit right now. Every time I see you you’re punching someone’s face in. I don’t know what’s going on with you but you’re going to end up in jail or dead and I won’t stand by and watch it happen. Just leave me alone okay?” I pulled away and he released his grip on me, standing motionless and confused.

"Tink, please let me explain. I just need a chance to talk to you. I could take you out somewhere. Maybe we could go up to the river and watch the boats?"

Something flickered inside my consciousness. It was like there was a memory that I'd forgotten locked somewhere deep inside me. But I couldn't quite reach it. There were boats and I was happy. The happiest I'd ever been. I shook my head to clear it and focused on Trick's face. "Why don't you take your girlfriend instead? Or is the dress code too intense for her?" I winced as I heard how bitchy I sounded.

Trick grimaced. "It's not how you think Tink; please give me the chance to explain? If you'd just let me talk to you then I'm sure I could fix this." He reached out to touch me again but I jerked away.

My anger was boiling in my veins now. "What exactly is it you think you can fix?"

He took my hands softly in his own. "You. Me. Us? I don't know Tink. Just please, let me try?" His eyebrows lifted expectantly.

"There is no 'us' Trick." He closed his eyes slowly and when he opened them again they were filled with a resigned sadness.

"There will always be an 'us' Tink. Always." He lifted my hand to his lips and placed a gentle kiss against my skin.

My eyes travelled the length of his arms and settled on the playing card tattooed on his flesh. "Huh." My fingers couldn't stop themselves as they traced the familiar outline. I had the same tattoo on my hip although at the time I couldn't understand why I wanted it, just that I'd begged Ben for it until he relented.

Trick smiled sadly. "I get it. You're not ready yet. But when you are, I'll be waiting." He squeezed my hand lightly before turning around and walking right out of the bar.

My legs took off with a mind of their own and I chased him outside, screaming his name into the street. He turned when he heard me and took a deep breath. "This doesn't change anything Trick. You still can't solve everything with your fists." My hands went to my hips as I stood in front of him defiantly.

"I know Tink. Something's just can't be solved." He shook his head softly before turning back and walking off into the night.

Chapter Three

I had purposefully picked up a few extra shifts at work to avoid explaining to Ben why I didn't want to go to McKinley's with him. I couldn't face Trick right now, I felt so angry with him and utterly confused. After two weeks, Ben stopped asking me to go anywhere with him and his normal casual playfulness had started to return. I knew things between him and Trick were strained and the last thing he needed was to hear about my troubles with him.

I came home late from work one night and heard voices in the front room. I was just about to push the door open to say hello when Trick's bassy tone reverberated through my very core. My whole body was telling me to step into that room but my brain was very firmly convinced that the best thing to do was go straight to bed. I stood frozen in front of the door, willing myself to turn around. The handle snapped down sharply and the door flew open, Trick's frame filling the empty space. He shouted something behind him as he stepped out and bumped straight in to me.

My eyes widened but I couldn't stop myself from stumbling backwards from the shock of the unexpected impact. Trick reached out quickly and scooped me up in his arms to prevent me from landing awkwardly. He plopped me safely down onto my feet and frowned. "Shit! Are you okay? Did I hurt you?"

I shook my head as Ben's face appeared above Trick's shoulder, full of concern. "Beth?" I stood completely still unable to speak, not sure of what I even wanted to say. My brother punched Trick lightly in the back. "What did you do now?"

Trick shrugged, moving out the way so Ben could examine me. "Nothing. I swear, I didn't see her there and nearly walked right in to her."

My brother was instantly running his hands over me looking for injuries until I finally managed to pull myself together. "I'm fine Ben, I'm fine." I held my hand out to stop him fussing and he relaxed slightly. "I was just going to say hi before I went to bed." I gestured towards the stairs desperately.

Ben frowned and was about to speak when Trick cut him off. "Come on Tink, you look exhausted. Let's get you to bed." Ben's face flashed full of rage but he allowed Trick to lead me upstairs and deposit me on the bed. I wanted to be able to direct my anger at him and unleash it until he felt even a small amount of the confusion I did but when he was sitting on my bed, my thoughts became blurry and tangled. My body wanted his more than it needed oxygen and my mind was in the gutter.

He sat down at my side and allowed himself a sad smile. Flicking off the light and pulling the top sheet over me, he stroked the hair back from my face. "Get some sleep Tink; you look like you need it." His touch sent shivers across my skin and I hated myself for wanting something I could never have.

He was more perceptive than he knew; I hadn't been able to sleep properly for weeks. As he pushed up to leave I put my hand on his knee gently making him pause. "Trick?"

He didn't answer for a minute, breathing heavily, his voice barely a whisper. "Yeah?"

"Will you hold me until I fall asleep?" As hard as it would be for me to deal with in the morning, I knew that I would never sleep without him next to me. I needed his contact and felt like I might die without it. Maybe it was the insomnia talking but I instinctively knew the only comfort I'd find would be in his arms.

He nodded and slipped in behind me, wrapping his arms around me and pulling my body against his. As soon as he had, I was overwhelmed with the feeling of how utterly right it felt, my eyelids suddenly feeling heavy and drooping closed almost immediately.

Trick laughed loudly, his eyes sparkling as the sun caught them. "Get down Tink, you'll hurt yourself."

I shook my head and continued on my path, placing one foot in front of the other on top of the high wall. "You'll always catch me if I fall right?"

His face was alight with pleasure. "Always baby. Always. Now get down here, I want to take you home."

I pushed off from the wall, dropping securely into his arms. "I love you Trick."

His big hand swept my hair from my face. "I love you too Tink." His eyes darted around the courtyard. "Y'know there's no-one around...." His voice was low and a growl rippled through his chest.

I sighed happily and wriggled until he placed me onto my feet again. My fingers went instantly to the fly of his jeans. "I wouldn't care even if there was." My cheeks hurt with the huge smile I couldn't take from my face.

Trick backed us up towards the wall, his lips on mine and his hands roaming under my skirt. His fingers pulled my panties to one side and delved inside me. "I love you so much, I want to live inside you." His kisses trailed down to my collarbone and my head rocked backwards while I struggled to free him from his jeans.

"Please Trick." I was begging now, desperate with need for him.

"Let go baby, I'll always catch you." My orgasm exploded around me like fireworks as he thrust inside of me and I knew there would never be any other man for me.

When I opened my eyes again, sunlight was streaming in through the window and Trick's scent was enveloping me completely. I sighed dreamily allowing the smell to dance across my senses delightfully while I recalled my dream. He was no longer lying next to me having fulfilled his obligation to help me sleep but the simple fact that he had done that for me and helped me feel completely rested for the first time in weeks made me smile right through my whole body. He didn't know it but he was forgiven for his crimes.

I danced down the stairs and into the kitchen. "You're in a better mood today. Sleep okay?"

I shrugged at Ben and put a mug down next to him so he could pour into mine as well as his own. I muttered my thanks and went to sit at the chair nearest the window so I could look outside and feel the sun on my face. "I'm going to ask Pip to come over tonight. Is that okay with you?"

Ben's lips pursed as he considered it. I had met Pip at work and since the first time she'd laid eyes on Ben she'd done everything possible to get naked with him. She was good fun and always liked to listen to me complain about how no man could ever match up to Trick so I knew she would be exactly what I needed. "Sure, I've got shit to do tonight anyway."

I frowned. "What sort of shit?"

"Nothing you need to worry about." He came and sat down across from me. "Are you okay Beth? I mean, I know there's been a lot going on lately but you can talk to me y'know?" He took a swig from his mug, cupping it protectively in both hands.

I picked at my thumbnail, not really sure how to start talking. "Things have just been weird lately and no-one will tell me what's going on. I dunno, just after Andy lied to me I guess it hurt so much more when you and Trick did it too." It was beyond emotional blackmail to say that to him but I wanted answers and was completely shameless.

Ben cleared his throat awkwardly. "We haven't been lying to you B, I promise. Just sometimes… they're some things that you don't need to know."

He looked uncomfortable as he fidgeted in his chair. "I don't think you should be the one to judge if I need to know something or not. It's obviously affecting me so I should know what's going on."

I could see him chewing the inside of his mouth anxiously like he used to do when we were younger. He looked anywhere but at me until he spoke. "Okay, how about we make a deal? I'll tell you what's going on if you answer me a question." He raised his eyebrows to me.

I tapped the table gently, weighing up my options. There were a number of things he could ask that I knew I wouldn't want to give him an answer to, the biggest of which was probably how last New Year his car ended up with a smashed windscreen but I was prepared to sacrifice one secret to find out what was going on between him and Trick and why everyone was acting so strangely around me all of a sudden. I nodded my consent. "Okay, shoot."

He swirled his coffee round in his mug a few times before asking me. "How do you feel about Trick?"

I gasped a little, having not expected that question in a million years. I took another sip of coffee and considered if I really wanted to tell him the truth. I knew Ben wouldn't judge me for how I felt but if things were awkward between them anyway then this wouldn't help the situation. I could never lie to my brother so I was faced with the truth or not answering and the desire to get my Nancy Drew on was just too strong. I settled on short and sweet, hoping to get it over with quickly. I looked Ben directly in the eyes so he would know there was no doubt in what I said. “I’m in love with him.”

Ben closed his eyes and swallowed. “I had a feeling you were going to say that.”

I took another huge gulp of coffee to steady my nerves but my hands were shaking. “Well now I have so return the favour.”

He pulled a cigarette from his jeans and lit it. Ben rarely smoked inside the house so I knew that whatever he was about to say was really affecting him. “Do you remember speaking to Trick at the funeral?”

My brow furrowed not understanding where we going with this. “Not really. Everyone was pretty distraught; I mostly remember crying and you carrying me to bed. I think I was pretty wasted.”

“Please Beth, this is important. You have to think about it.” Ben was acting strangely now with an intensity to him that I never normally saw.

I rested my head on the back of the chair and tried to remember what had been one of the most painful times in my life. Watching Trick shatter into a million pieces in front of my very eyes when I couldn't do anything to stop it was just too hard. I felt my eyes welling up with tears just trying to remember that day. I wiped my sleeve across my face and shook my head. "I can't Ben, it's too hard." Annie had been everything to Trick and his heartbreak was mine too.

He took another drag of his cigarette and exhaled sharply. "I'm not going to give you the answer. All I'll say is that he made good on his promise to me and now he's working on yours." He pushed his chair back and walked out of the room, clearly annoyed with me.

I spent the afternoon wandering around the house trying desperately to remember but nothing came to me. I hoped that Pip would be able to help me decipher all the crazy clues that were being left around for me.

She bounced up and down with excitement when I told her, clapping her hands over her face. "Oh my God, it's like a real mystery. Okay, we've got the breadcrumbs and now we have to follow them to Granny's house. You must have spoken to him at this funeral right?" Pip was a few years younger than me with short blonde spiky hair. The overall effect made her look like a crazy pixie. If a crazy pixie had loads of tattoos and got overly excited about any situation.

I finished my glass of wine and poured myself another, surmising that alcohol was bound to help the situation. "Yeah I think so." I grimaced.

"So pretend like you lost your keys and you had to go back to the last place you found them. Just think about it, you spoke to him so where were you, how were you sitting, and what were you wearing? If you pick out the details then you'll get there no problem." Pip's smile was full of encouragement.

She was perfectly silent and still while I searched my brain for answers, closing my eyes and trying to envisage the scene. "Okay, so I was really upset and went and sat outside on a wall. It was definitely a brick wall because I was wearing a knee length black dress and the next day I had little scrapes on my thighs from the brickwork." I traced my things with my thumbs, consumed by the memory of the feeling of the grazes on my skin. "Trick came out for a smoke and saw me and came and sat next to me."

Pip squeezed my hands comfortingly. "I put my arms around his neck and wanted to tell him how sorry I was for him but the words just wouldn't come out. He rested his head on mine and looked into my eyes and said….. arrrgghh! I can't remember!" My eyes flew open and I downed my wine in a single swallow.

Pip rubbed my back supportively. "It's okay Beth. You got real close then, try again." She crossed her legs on the sofa and pulled a full meditation pose, encouraging me to do the same and centre myself. I mirrored her and concentrated on my breathing. In. Out. In. Out. In. Out.

Like lightning splitting a rock, it came to me with a sudden crack. I leapt off the sofa and my hands flew to my face with the shock. “Holy shit! I remember.”

Pip jumped up with me and hugged me tightly. “Great, what did he say?” Her eyes were wide with anticipation.

I sat back down, my heart thumping hard through my rib cage. “He said ‘one day I’m going to wake up and not feel so sad. Things will be better and I’ll not be carrying all this shit around with me and I’ll be able to be the man you need me to be. When that day comes I promise you, I’ll ask Ben’s permission and then I’m coming back for you. You and I will be together forever.”

Pip’s mouth fell open. She stood up and waved her hands in front of her slowly. “How. The. Fuck. Did you forget that? That would be burned on my mind forever. Seriously? What is wrong with you?” She grabbed my shoulders and shook me slightly.

I swallowed hard. “I have no fucking idea. What do I do now?” I felt completely numb inside.

Pip grabbed my phone from the table and threw it on to my lap. “Err, you call him you idiot.”

I looked down at my phone as if it was a contagious disease. “I can’t.”

Chapter Four

As soon as Ben got home he took one look at me and swept me up in a gentle embrace, stroking my head and whispering to me. “Oh B, I’m so sorry, I should have told you but you needed to get there on your own. I just didn’t know how you felt about him and I was worried about you. I don’t think he’s good enough for you right now. I don’t want to see you get hurt. I’m sorry.”

I pulled away slightly and stared at him. “What do you mean you don’t think he’s good enough for me?” The urge to defend Trick to my brother was utterly overwhelming.

Ben smiled awkwardly. “Oh come on Beth, I know you have feelings for him but even you’ve got to admit you could do better.”

I shook my head. “In what way?” Something about the way he was speaking was really making me angry and I had an urge to slap him but I didn’t know why.

He frowned. “Err, let’s see… the fighting, the drinking, the women, the lack of career and direction, the complete inability to share his feelings. Basically he’s a fucking mess and I don’t really want to watch him destroy you.”

I blinked, searching Ben’s face for some sign that he was joking. “Is this why you were fighting? Did you say no?”

He released me and flung his hands out in frustration. “Oh course I said no. But who the fuck am I to keep two people who love each other apart? I’d just rather it wasn’t happening.”

He kicked the skirting board heavily. “Well it’s not happening is it? Because neither one of us wants to hurt you.” I spat the words at him, blaming him for all my misery. I didn't really understand what was happening between Trick and my brother but I could tell from the way he was speaking that Ben was to blame somehow.

Ben leaned back against the wall and sighed. “It’s not about me B, it’s about you. He will consume you until there’s nothing left and when he realises things can’t be the way he wants them, he’ll leave you and you’ll break into tiny little pieces and I won’t know how to put you back together again.” A look of agony crossed his face. Ben always worried about me but this was past the line of overprotective even for him.

I slumped down to the floor trying to absorb everything he’d said. “But I love him.” I had to sob through every word, feeling as if I’d already dated and lost Trick in the space of five minutes.

He shuffled round and sat beside me. “I know you do and that’s why I’m not going to stop you. I just wish you'd think carefully about going through this again.”

I frowned on instinct. "Again? What are you talking about? Trick is nothing like Andy. I don’t know why you won’t give him a chance." Shouting came naturally now, like I'd opened a floodgate of anger inside me.

Ben squeezed his eyes shut tightly and knelt down so he was level with me. "Oh babe there's so many things I wish I could tell you." His palm ran across his stubble and when he looked at me his face showed me how much he was holding back.

"Just be honest with me Ben. Please?" I knew he was hiding so much and I couldn't understand why. "I wish I could babe, I really do." Ben's hand squeezed my arm before he stood up and left me alone to drown in my own misery and confusion, eventually making my way up to bed with a heavy heart.

The first thing to hand was a saucepan so I grabbed it and sent it sailing towards my brother's head. He ducked just in time to escape losing an eye. "What the fuck Beth? Will you calm down before you actually kill me?"

I snatched up a plate and chucked that too. "No. You can't stop me doing this Ben. I love him. I'm moving in with him. End of story. You're not my dad!" The only thing left on the counter was a tea towel so I put some extra force behind it when I launched it towards him.

"Don't you think I know that?" He rocked back on his heels and sighed in frustration. When he spoke again, he'd managed to control his temper and his tone was much calmer. "Jesus Beth. I'm just worried about you. What if something happens? I've always been there before. If you leave then I won't be able to keep an eye on you."

Trick motioned from the doorway. "May I interject?"

Ben shouted no and I shouted yes. I glared at my brother and turned to Trick. "Of course baby. Go ahead." I gave him a sweet smile that promised lots of wonderful things later if he'd take my side.

Trick moved cautiously into the kitchen and looked my brother right in the eye. "Ben. Believe me. The last thing I want is for anything to happen to her. She'll be safe with me. I promise you. I'll kill myself before I let anything bad happen. She's my whole fucking world."

I made my way over to Trick and wrapped my arms around him. "I love you so much baby." The emotion was so raw and it was all I could do to cling on and let Trick's energy flow into me.

He looked down at me and bent in to brush my lips with his. "I love you too."

Ben's shoulders drooped in defeat. "Fine. Do whatever you want. Just remember I will be the one shouting 'I told you so' from the rooftops when this goes horribly wrong." He held my gaze firmly. "It will. I know it."

I spent at least a week walking around like a complete zombie. I went to work and smiled politely and then came home to stare at the TV until it was time for bed. Lather, rinse, repeat. Having spent so long being in a state of unrequited love with a man who it appeared did in fact love me back but hadn't found it in himself to tell me, was just a complete mind fuck. Also, Ben was always at the forefront of my mind. He had put me above all else and I didn't want to make him miserable at the price of my own happiness but he was keeping something from me and it nagged at me like an itchy scab. I was convinced that Ben's feelings on the matter were the reason Trick had kept his distance and even the thought of going directly against the very thing my brother had warned me about just seemed utterly wrong. Sure there had been times when he'd told me to eat something disgusting or put my hand in something vile but he had never given me bad advice on anything that mattered. Not listening to him now, when I was standing at the crossroads of such a huge decision just felt ridiculous.

It didn't help that every time I closed my eyes I kept having really vivid dreams about a life with Trick. In my dream state we lived a million adventures and he loved me right down into his soul. Whenever I woke I felt disappointed that they were nothing but my imagination and they only served to make me more miserable.

No matter how hard I'd tried over the years to get past my feelings for Trick, it had proved impossible. Every date I'd ever had was always compared to him and every kiss I'd ever experienced had never lived up to what I'd imagined kissing Trick would be like. I was hopelessly head over heels for him but deep down I knew that Ben had a point. I would never be Annie and in the same way my boyfriends were compared to Trick, I would be compared to her and would always be found wanting. She didn't leave him or cheat on him, she died. The perfect memories he had of her would never go away and I would never be good enough. Eventually if he didn't push me away himself then the anxiety I felt about it would ultimately have me running toward the nearest exit.

I knew I had to get over him somehow and as my mother always used to say 'to get over a man, you have to get under another one'. She'd certainly done enough of that when our dad left and occasionally it felt like we had a revolving front door instead of a normal one. I resolved that I was going to go to work with a real smile on my face and let the universe show me the answer. If a hot single man appeared in front of me tonight then that was definitely a sign as far as I was concerned.

It took four miserable and exhausting hours where my neck almost went into spasm, craning repeatedly towards the door before the universe sent me my sign. In fact I'd become so fed up with the lack of any type of hot single man that I'd almost stopped looking and actually tripped over him and fell into his lap while attempting to make my way back through the crowds to the bar. I raised my eyebrows in surprise and apology as he flashed me a beautiful smile. "Wow, who knew that tonight I would have girls falling over themselves to get to me?"

He helped me up and dusted me down gently. "Err…hi. Sorry about that." My cheeks flushed as he grinned at me.

"It is absolutely no problem at all. In fact, anytime you want to make my year again then by all means, drop right down." He gestured to his lap with a flourish and I stifled a giggle. "I'm Leo." He held his hand out to me and as I took it, I noticed the edge of a tattoo peeking out from under the sleeve of his smartly pressed shirt. He didn't look like the normal sort of guy my brother hung out with, all smart trousers and shiny shoes.

"Beth. Pleased to meet you Leo." I couldn't help but grin goofily at him as he ran his hand through his thick messy blonde hair.

"The pleasure is entirely mine. Can I get your number?" He maintained eye contact with me as he spoke, unlike most of the guys I talked to who found their eyes incapable of looking anywhere but at my breasts.

I nodded once, more to the universe than him. "Sure." He tilted his head slightly with a grin as if he had been expecting a brush off but then reached into his pocket and handed over his phone trustingly.

I bit my lip as I entered my number and handed it back. “Thanks. What time do you finish?”

I shrugged. “About three probably.”

“Okay, I shall call you at half past and say goodnight.” His cheeks lifted with a smile and I had to fight back a desire to curtsey. I nodded quickly and practically ran away from him, not wanting to break the spell. I didn’t see him leave but he wasn’t around when I next went out to collect glasses.

From two onwards, I felt like I was on a countdown, rushing around to get everything cleared away. Dan raised an eyebrow at me as I upturned chairs onto the newly cleared tables with an unprecedented vigour. At exactly three, I sighed heavily knowing there was still at least another hour’s worth of work to do. Dan leant on my shoulder with his elbow. “Go on, I can see you have somewhere to be.” He gestured towards the door.

“Are you serious?” At that precise moment, Dan was my hero.

"You owe me big time." I kissed his cheek enthusiastically and promised him a thousand shifts covered and various other things as I sprinted out of the door.

I made it back to my room for twenty past, throwing myself down on the bed and catching my breath. I made a mental note to thank Ben for being an overprotective brother and letting me have his car tonight. I sat and stared at my phone and as the display flicked over to half past, it started ringing. I grabbed it up eagerly and answered.

"Hey Beth. How was work?" His voice sounded even more deep and delicious over the phone than in person.

I lay on my front and let my calves sail into the air, crossing my ankles over. "Crazy busy but it's all good. How was your night?"

"It's got a lot better in the last minute or so." My heart melted a little with the sweetness of him. "So, can I ask you something?"

"Sure. Ask away." I felt like a giggly teenager again.

"When can I take you out?"

I rolled over onto my side with a smile. "Tomorrow night's free for me if you are?"

"Hmm, you mean tonight right?" His voice was deep and seductive making parts of me pulse and throb.

I blinked, having never thought about it that way before. "Yeah, I guess so."

"Okay, then sure, I can do that. Shall I pick you up or do you want to meet somewhere in case I'm a creepy stalker guy?"

I giggled playfully. "Good point. I'll meet you. Just tell me where."

"Hmmm, Okay, how about eight at Westley's. Do you know it?"

Of course I knew it; they had the best food for miles. "Yep, see you at eight?"

"Great. Good night Beth."

"Good night Leo." I hung up and lay back on my pillow. I knew it was ridiculous to get all giddy over a first date but just the thought that I could be with someone who wouldn't cause my brother immense stress and pain made me feel so much lighter.

Chapter Five

I skipped into the front room at half seven fully dressed. I wasn't much of a dress person but I'd managed to dig out a long sleeved black number that had a Marilyn Monroe style skirt and a diamond cut in the centre to show some cleavage. Despite being a far cry from my normal jeans and jumpers, I felt quite pretty. “Can you drop me in town quickly pleeeeeease?” I flashed my best begging smile.

Ben looked me over with a frown. “Where are you going?”

“Out.” I folded my arms in mock stubborn determination.

Ben shook his head. “No. No fucking way are you going out with him dressed like that.” He stood up and started to lead me back upstairs.

"What? What's wrong with… wait. What? How do you know about Leo?" I stopped still and turned to look at Ben who was now as completely confused as I was.

"Leo? Who the fuck is Leo?"

I shook my head. "My date. Why? Who did you think I was meeting? Oh." I pursed my lips at the thought that Ben had presumed I was meeting Trick.

He took a step back and looked me over appraisingly. "You look great. Come on, let's go." He grabbed his keys and headed out to the car with me following behind in utter confusion.

As he started the engine I looked at him. "What's wrong with what I'm wearing?"

He snorted. "Nothing B, you look good."

"But not good enough for Trick?" I frowned and played with the hem of my dress.

"No. Not at all. Too good for Trick." He sighed and stared out at the road. As he pulled up outside Westley's he smiled sadly at me. "Have a good time and call me if you need a lift home okay? I'll stay up until you get in." I had never said 'don't wait up' to my brother and had never found cause to either. I kissed him softly before getting out and pushing the door shut behind me.

Leo was waiting for me as I entered and he held out his arm and led me to our table, pulling out my chair before I sat down. "You look beautiful." I blushed at the compliment and I quickly found that unlike the other guys I'd dated, he was not only full of compliments but also really easy to talk to. We covered all the basics before dessert and had similar tastes in movies, music and books. He pointed his fork at me. "So what's your absolute favourite movie?"

I didn't have to think about it. "Fight Club."

Leo frowned. "That's not really a chick flick is it? Why do you like it so much?"

I smiled, pleased that I'd managed to surprise him. "I like the idea that you could be a completely different person and not even know it. Like another half of yourself is buried deep inside fighting to get out. Also, I really like the *Jackism's.* They help me with my thoughts."

Leo studied me carefully before sniggering. "Okay, tell me. What's a *Jackism*?" He air quoted with his fingers.

I shook my head, unable to comprehend someone who didn't understand this indelible part of modern filmmaking. "Y'know; *I am Jack's raging bile duct. I am Jack's smirking revenge?*" I held my hands up in a questioning gesture.

He raised an eyebrow and pursed his lips in a tight smile. "Can't say that I do but I'm sure gonna find out."

My leg shook slightly under the table, pleased with his desire to know more about me. Something about him made me feel like I constantly needed to win his approval. It was kind of hot in a very weird way that I couldn't quite understand. As I tucked into my chocolate brownie, I felt confident enough to delve a little deeper into his life, pointing to him with my spoon. "So, how come a nice guy like you has so much ink?"

He smirked. “How do you know I have a lot of tattoos?”

“I can see the edges of at least two poking out of your sleeves and there’s no way you’d have them done first so you must either have two full sleeves or at least a chest plate.”

“I’m impressed. You sure know a lot about tattoos. You have any?”

I grinned, satisfied to have impressed him. “Deflect much?”

He coughed at my comment, suppressing a chuckle. “I used to ride Motocross. I was pretty good too, probably would have made a career out of it but I shattered my pelvis and couldn’t ride again.” He shrugged like it was no big deal as I frowned in sympathy.

Realisation crossed my face. “Wait. You’re Leo McCarthy?” He nodded with an embarrassed smile. “You were amazing. Like out of this world.” I grimaced realising that the last thing he probably wanted to hear was someone going on about the best time of his life that he would never go back to.

“Thanks. I’m even more impressed now. So how come you know about all this stuff?”

I rolled my eyes. “Twin brother.” It was a statement of fact. There was nothing about any interest of Ben’s that I hadn’t had rammed down my throat endlessly until I knew every single last detail.

Leo grinned. “Nice. So… do you have any tattoos?”

I nodded and smiled coyly. “A couple.” Ben had done them both and I loved them. I had a smattering of stars around my ankle and an ace of spades on my hip.

He licked his lips seductively. “I’d like to see them some time.” The insinuation in his tone was followed up by a slightly creepy full body eye sweep.

I suddenly felt incredibly uncomfortable. We had taken a rambling walk across the fields to get to it but yet here we were already arriving at the subject of nakedness. My mouth felt dry and my breathing was really shallow. It took all my energy just to focus on not throwing up. “I…. errr….I….” I stammered and had no idea what to say.

Leo nodded slowly. “Not right now or anything. Don’t panic.” He grinned again and I looked down at my chocolate cake, nudging it awkwardly with my spoon.

“I should call my brother and get him to pick me up.” I pulled out my phone and Leo just nodded.

Ben answered on the first ring. “I’m on my way, be there in five.” He hung up and I couldn’t help but feel ridiculously relieved.

Leo saw it too and took my hand in his. “Will you see me again?”

I frowned. “I don’t think so Leo. I’m sorry.” I smiled pathetically and practically ran through the door when I saw Ben pull up.

He undid his seatbelt as I frantically scrambled to connect mine. “Where is he? Do I need to go and sort this out?” His hand was already on the door handle.

I shook my head furiously, my hand grasping onto his arm in a futile attempt to stop him going anywhere. “No Ben. Nothing like that, just take me home please.” He leant over and kissed me on the cheek before driving home.

All I wanted to do was go to bed and sleep so I wouldn’t have to think about what a complete mess I was but Ben wasn’t having any of it. He pulled me into the kitchen and sat me down before pouring me a vodka and placing it gently in front of me. “Tell me what happened Beth because what I’m imagining right now is gonna make me want to go and break his legs.”

I took a sip and sighed. “It’s nothing like that, I promise. I just freaked out when he started talking about stuff.”

Ben leaned forward. “What stuff?”

I shrugged. “Y’know? Sex and stuff.” Sex wasn't a topic I was all that comfortable with at the best of times.

Ben frowned and then let a laugh escape his lips. "But why did that freak you out? It's not like you've never… oh." He blinked in realisation. "Shit B, sorry."

One side of my mouth turned upwards in a smile. "It's okay, just sometimes guys want more than I'm prepared to give them and I don't really know how to handle it." Talking about sex with my brother was really awkward.

He raised his eyebrows and studied me. "It's because of Trick isn't it?"

I exhaled deeply and looked at my hands, the tiniest slither of a tear falling from my eyelid. "I guess I always figured that when the time came, it would be him."

Ben sucked in a sharp breath between his teeth. "Shit. I'm a fucking bastard aren't I?" I frowned and shook my head. "Yes I am. I've got no right to stand between you two. I just want to protect you B, you know that right?"

I swallowed. "Ben… All the things you said… you were right. It would be awful for me if we broke up; there wouldn't be any coming back from that for me." I took his hand and squeezed my encouragement of his disapproval.

He looked into my eyes for a long time before he spoke. "Sometimes B, the payoff is worth the gamble." I wanted to cry at his words but he already had his phone out and was making a call. I frowned at him for being so rude until I followed the conversation. "I'm coming over, get dressed… you better be alone you cunt or I'll kick your fucking ass." He looked at me and then gestured to the door. "Come on, we're going out."

I found myself almost helplessly following behind him to the car and when I got in to the seat, I glared at him. "Why is it that you keep dragging me to places when I don't want to go?"

He sniggered. "Trust me; this is a place you want to be going." We drove in silence until we pulled up outside Trick's house. My body was singing its approval at the promised proximity but my mind was cycling through a thousand thoughts a second and so far 'run away, run away' was winning. “Have you got your phone?” I nodded. “Good. If you need me, call me. I love you.” He leaned over and opened my door wide for me while unfastening my seatbelt with his other hand. I stared at him in complete shock for a minute but he only pointed his eyebrows towards the path. I sighed and got out on to shaky legs, Ben pulling away before I’d barely closed the door.

As I walked up the path, Trick’s door opened and he stood there with a look of complete confusion on his face. I shrugged and smiled whimsically. “Delivery?” Now I was here I figured I should at least go inside.

He laughed and opened the door wide for me so I could enter. “Can I get you a drink or something?” I nodded and he went into the kitchen while I plopped myself down on the sofa. He came and sat down next to me and held out a can of pop. We simultaneously cracked the ring pulls making us both giggle nervously. "So?"

He looked far more anxious than I felt and I knew that if I didn't get everything out immediately then I'd never be able to rebuild the confidence to say it later. "I wanted to apologise." Sitting so close to him only fortified the feeling that my life was incomplete without him.

He shook his head. "What for?"

"I forgot. What you said at the funeral, I forgot. But I remember now." Trick visibly exhaled in relief. "The truth is Trick, I'm a complete mess and you're not any less dysfunctional but I can't stop myself from being hopelessly in love with you." His eyes widened. "I know that if anything happens between us, you will end up completely breaking me apart but you've already ruined me for any other man so I guess what I'm saying is.... What I'm saying is... fuck it." I shrugged.

The silence stretched between us as he stared at me, a wealth of emotions flashing across his face. He leaned forward excruciatingly slowly and touched my lips with his. When I didn't resist, he increased the pressure and my body tingled in the knowledge that it was finally getting what it had been craving. He had barely slipped his tongue into my mouth when he yanked himself backwards. I lurched forward, desperate for him to touch me again.

He smiled so sweetly that I thought I heard birds chirping. "I don't want to fuck this up again. Let's do it properly okay?" I blinked a few times unsure if he was building himself up to rejecting me. "How about a date first and then we can work up to the kissing and stuff?" He rubbed his neck nervously. I nodded and he took my hand, bringing it to his lips to kiss it softly. "I love you too by the way. Just in case that wasn't clear before."

Chapter Six

Trick offered to take me home and I practically floated up the stairs to bed while he spoke to Ben and explained what we'd agreed. We had a proper date set for the weekend and I wanted to go to sleep quickly so the next day would come sooner. I checked my phone before closing my eyes and saw I had eight missed calls from Leo and one from Andy. I sighed and threw my phone onto my bedside table hoping that they wouldn't call again if I didn't answer.

I slept like a log and when I finally opened my eyes, it was necessary to peel the pillowcase from my face where it had embedded itself and was slowly becoming fused to my skin. I trudged downstairs to make some tea and Ben grinned at me when I entered the kitchen. I flipped him off before pouring hot water over a teabag and leaning back against the work surface. I stared at him blearily. "Why are you so fucking cheerful this morning?" I took a sip of my tea and rubbed my eyes.

Ben shrugged with a smirk. "No reason. The real question is why aren't you looking cheerier? Bad dreams?" His forehead scrunched into concern.

I shook my head and tried to remember if I had dreamt about anything at all but there was nothing there. "Nope. Just feeling like shit. I might go back to bed actually. What time is it?"

Ben raised an eyebrow at me and I shot both of mine back at him sarcastically. "Beth, I've been to work already. It's gone six."

I stared at him unable to quite comprehend what he was saying, convinced that he must be winding me up. "Fuck off, what time is it really?" He sniggered and looked back at his glass with a sigh. "No way is it that late." I stomped over to him and grabbed his phone off the table in front of him and flicked the screen lock off. I looked between Ben and his phone like I was caught in some sort of bizarre sitcom. “Shit.” Slumping down into a chair, I dropped his phone back on the table.

“Are you okay?” I shook my head, not really knowing what to say. “Seriously B, if this is what one night with Trick does to you, maybe you should stay away.” His face was deadly serious.

“Fuck off twat face. It wasn’t like that.” I thought about the date Trick had promised to take me on at the weekend and felt flutters spread up through my tummy.

Ben grabbed his phone and stood up. “Whatever you say B. I’ve gotta go but call me if you need me okay? I’m worried about you.” I gestured that I would but that he should still go and he only lingered in the doorway for a moment before closing the front door behind him.

Before I could even think about getting dressed or trying to work out how I’d slept the whole day away, the doorbell rang. I pushed up from the table and wandered over to the door, looking through the peephole first like

Ben had insisted I always do if I was alone in the house. Andy stood there, leaning casually with one hand against the woodwork. “I know you’re there Beth. Open up please.” He didn’t sound angry with me like the night he’d stormed away from me so I sighed heavily and opened the door. Andy smirked sexily. “Hey. Can we talk?” He looked up at me through his lashes, causing me to roll my eyes as I stepped aside to let him enter.

I resumed my seated position at the table and he slid into the chair next to me. “What do you want Andy?” My tone was brusque and probably not the best way to stay civil but I just couldn't be bothered with him today.

He frowned. “No need for hostilities. I just came to talk.”

I bit my lip, trying to keep in all the things I wanted to shout at him. “Talk then.”

“I miss you. I think we should give it another shot.” He rolled his tongue around his lips nervously as he exhaled deeply.

A deep laugh burst out of me making a ‘pa’ sound and throwing me into a mini coughing fit. “What? Are you joking?” I couldn't believe the nerve of the man.

He shook his head. “No, not at all. I figure it’s the least I deserve from you.” He gestured to his black eyes with the tips of his fingers.

I waved my hand in disbelief. “Andy, that wasn’t my fault. If you hadn’t cheated on me then my friends wouldn’t have wanted to hurt you. I don’t owe you shit.”

He pulled his phone out and pressed a few buttons before handing it over to me. I took it but didn’t look at it. “I thought you might say that so I thought I’d show you this. Look at that and tell me that cheating is a deal breaker.” Andy had a smug self-satisfied grin now and I felt extremely nervous to look down at the screen. He nodded towards it. “Go on, look. I took that this morning.”

I lifted the phone to my eye line and instantly regretted it. I could tell from the tattoos across his naked back that it was definitely Trick but I had no idea who the blonde he was obviously balls deep in was. I tossed the phone back to Andy. “You didn’t take that this morning.”

He let out a breathy laugh and nodded. “Hate to tell you this Beth, but I totally did. He’ll never love you like you want him to. You know it, I know it and the whole fucking world knows it. Just come back to me and we’ll forget the whole thing ever happened.” He reached out for my hand and I jerked it away, pushing back on my chair so the legs squeaked irritatingly across the tiles.

“Just get the fuck out Andy.” He tried to reach for me again but now I was standing, I practically sprinted to the other side of the kitchen. “Get the fuck out!” I screeched at him and the shock had him to his feet and towards the door.

“Just think about it” he pleaded with me before slipping outside and clicking the door shut behind him. I instantly sank to the floor and put my head in my hands.

I wanted to cry but I wasn’t really sure what I was upset about. I knew I should be mad at Trick but I just couldn't believe after what we'd said last night that he'd do anything like that. Andy was always trying to stir things up in some way and I was so annoyed at him for doing it now, after we'd broken up. He had every reason to lie to me if he thought it would either get me back or hurt Trick so I figured I just needed to hear it from the man himself. I pulled myself up and stumbled up the stairs, still feeling sleepy and slightly woozy.

As I sat on the edge of the bed, I saw Leo had called a few times this morning but I just clicked ignore and scrolled through to Trick's number. After each ring, my heart thumped a little harder until he eventually answered after seven rings.

"Hey?" He sounded flustered and a little annoyed with me.

"Sorry, is this a bad time?"

He cleared his throat and I heard a door closing. "No, what's up?" He was distracted and non-committal like someone was there with him.

My Own Worst Enemy

"I wanted to ask you something." I curled a piece of hair in my fingers nervously.

"Okay." His monosyllabic responses were making me feel sick with anxiety.

I released a giggle, trying to lighten my mood. "This is going to sound ridiculous but did you have sex with someone today?" I laughed again at the end, hoping that he would start laughing too and tell me how stupid I was being.

There was silence; the sort of silence that stretches out in front of you until you want to throw yourself off the top of a very tall building. I held my breath, waiting for him to say something, anything at all to alleviate the panic that was building inside of me. "Tink….I…." My eyes widened and I hit the end call button, hurling my phone across the room.

My mouth was agape and I looked around my room in complete shock. My breath quickened rapidly and my heart constricted to a point where pain was actually rippling across my chest and up my arm. My vision blurred and I felt my whole body tip forward.

When I opened my eyes, I was lying on the carpet and it was pitch black in my room. I slid across the floor to lean against my bed and that's when the tears started to fall. I actually felt like my heart was breaking and I wondered how long it would take to get a new one on a transplant list. My bedroom door flew open and Ben stood in the empty space staring at me frantically with wild eyes. As soon as my gaze met his, he threw himself onto the floor next to me and pulled me into an embrace.

"Jesus B, what the fuck? Has something happened?"

I tried to speak but all that came out were the most pathetic little sniffs. I hadn't cried as much in my whole life as I had in the last few weeks. I felt like my chest was going to implode in on itself from the agony I felt inside me. Ben held my cheeks gently in his palms and seemed at a complete loss as to what to say to me. "Trick…" It was the only word I could manage to push out of my lips and as soon as it was out, Ben's face instantly darkened.

He shot upwards like I'd slapped him and smashed his fist against the wall, denting the plasterboard with a heavy thud. "Fuck!" He let out a furious scream and then put his hand out in signal to me. "Stay there a minute." He stormed out of the room and I tried to push off the floor and go after him but the most I could manage was rolling my head to the side. I felt terribly weak and tired, sleep threatening to consume me in rolling waves. I could hear Ben's voice talking in the distance but it was like he was at the end of a long tunnel and it sounded muffled. It felt so difficult just to blink that eventually I gave up completely and just closed my eyes.

"I can't believe how bad you are at this." Trick chuckled as he pulled me into his arms and I let him hold me tightly.

"It's not my fault. Ice skating is completely unnatural. Feet should be on the floor at all times." I

looked down at my skates and wrinkled my nose at the sight of my soaking wet jeans. "You could at least have caught me when I fell over."

He pushed me back slightly, his lips curling upwards. "No freaking way. You are hilarious when you're falling over." Leaning down, he pecked the end of my nose with a soft kiss. "You want to give up and go home?"

"No, I feel like I need to accomplish something for all these bruises I'm gonna have tomorrow."

Trick turned suddenly, sliding me along the ice until he had me pressed up against the edge of the rink. Looking into my eyes, he bent in so close that I was inhaling nothing but carbon dioxide. "You want me to kiss them better?"

My skin vibrated to his frequency and I could think of nothing better than letting him kiss me all over. My fingers curled into the seam of his jacket and I tugged him closer so our lips could finally meet. The feel of his tongue against mine made me want to melt into him like the ice all over my clothes. He moved back first, his grey eyes dancing with possibility. "Will you at least show me how to go forward?"

"I'll show you anything you want Tink." His fingers wrapped around mine and I let the warmth seep into me as he led me round patiently. Never willing to give up on me.

Chapter Seven

I opened my eyes and knew something was wrong. The sheets wrapped around me felt unnaturally soft and the smell in the room was clinical and a far step from home. Someone grabbed my hand and I looked down to see my brother rubbing his eyes with his free hand, a sad smile stretching across his lips. “Hey.”

I tried to speak but my mouth felt like it was full of cotton wool. I prised my tongue from the roof of my mouth and Ben reached out to hand me a plastic cup of water. I lifted it to my lips and as I drank I saw my wrists were wrapped tightly with thick sterile bandages. I handed the cup back to Ben with a frown. “What the fuck happened?”

He looked like he was fighting back tears as he spoke, his voice barely a whisper. “You did it again B. I came home and found you." His face paled and it looked like the memory alone would make him throw up.

I shook my head and it felt like my skull was completely empty, only a tiny pea sized brain rattling around in the cavernous space. "What are you talking about? What did I do?"

Ben bit his lip and closed his eyes, swallowing sharply. When he opened them again, a tear rolled down his cheek and I saw his whole face was streaked and puffy. He ran one hand through his hair and squeezed my hand with his other. "You have to remember B, please try."

I lay my head back against the pillow and closed my eyes. I remembered speaking to Trick and hurling my phone and then sitting back against the bed. I thought I'd passed out from a panic attack and then Ben came home. I knew there had to be something I was missing so I tried to concentrate on the moment when I couldn't breathe and then everything seemed to be okay again. Slowly it started coming back to me. I'd crawled across the floor to the bathroom and pulled myself up on the sink. I remembered how the cool porcelain had felt against my skin as I reached out to open the bathroom cabinet and then how the scissors had felt in my palm; heavy and intoxicating, like they held all the answers. I remembered how the first slice into my wrist had been so comforting. I opened my eyes and stared at Ben. “Fuck.”

He bent his head low and kissed my hand softly. “I love you B, I’m so sorry I didn’t stay. I should have known something was wrong when you slept all day.”

I thought back to my long sleep and another memory came to the surface. The screen on my phone had missed calls from Leo and Andy and the distress it caused me had me sitting on the toilet seat with the scissors in my hand. That night I’d carved a chunk out of my thigh and barely made it back to my bed before I blacked out from the pain. “How long?” The words caught in my throat and I had to splutter them out. He'd said 'again' so this had been going on for longer than I realised.

My Own Worst Enemy

Ben looked away from me with a sharp breath. "A long time baby, a long time."

I felt numb inside like my own mind had betrayed me. I couldn't remember if I'd done anything like this before but I didn't doubt my brother's sincerity. "Where am I?" I looked around the room and had no idea how I'd even got here, yet another sign that I couldn't trust myself and my own judgement.

Ben sighed, his features contorted in agony. "Think baby, please. You've been here before. Please, try and remember." He looked completely heart broken and I wanted to hold him and tell him everything would be alright.

I scoured the room for clues but nothing came to mind. I frowned and turned my head towards the window wondering what time it was. The sunny yellow curtains caught my eye and a flash of recognition flew across my brain. "Risemoor." Ben nodded, relief flooding across his face. I had been here before; it was a mental health facility and if Ben had brought me here then things must be really bad. I swallowed. “I want to go home.”

He nodded. “I know baby, I know. Not just yet okay? I’ll come by and visit you tomorrow.” He kissed my hand again and allowed himself one last devastated look in my direction before he made his way dejectedly out of the room.

The door opened again a few moments later and a casually dressed woman bustled in, a tight smile stretched across her lips. “I’m glad you’re awake Beth. Everyone was worried about you. Do you think you can make it to group?”

I nodded and swung my legs out of bed as she handed me a t-shirt and a pair of jeans. I knew her name was Cathy but I had no idea where the knowledge of that came from. As I trailed behind her down the corridor, I let my arm stretch out and brush the walls with my fingertips. I imagined walking through a tall grassy meadow and feeling the vegetation scrape against my skin as the sun beat down on my face.

My Own Worst Enemy

I made my way into a large mostly empty room where there was a small circle of chairs already inhabited by an eclectic mix of people with one thing in common. The haunted look in their eyes was evident across each one of them. I took the only free seat, curling my knees up to my chest and resting my head on my hands. Cathy began to speak but I didn't hear her. All I could think is how on Earth I had managed to get to this point. As if she could read my mind, Cathy began saying my name softly. I glanced up at her and blinked making it clear that I hadn't heard a question that I needed to respond to.

"Can you tell us what happened yesterday Beth?" She smiled sadly in my direction and everyone turned to look at me.

I shook my head. "Not really, I cut myself I guess." I pulled at a thread on the edge of one of my bandages.

"And how did that make you feel?"

I stared at my wrists trying to recall what was going through my mind at the time but I couldn't shake the knowledge that there was so much I couldn't remember. I just shrugged and Cathy stared at me for a long time, silently willing me to open up. Once she realised she wasn't going to get anything else, she moved on.

The next few days were a blur. I went between meals and group sessions as a hazy fog descended over me and the more I searched my mind for answers, the further away the truth seemed to get. I'd heard some of the other patients talking about Saturday being visiting day but I didn't know if Ben would show up or if he would be too angry with me to come and see me. The hurt and sadness in his face when I'd last seen him had lingered with me and made it difficult to sleep. I settled on curling up on my bed and trying to sleep so I wouldn't feel so bad when he didn't arrive, at least unconscious I wouldn't know for sure that he hadn't shown up.

I heard my door open and felt my mattress depress as someone settled themselves beside me. I reluctantly opened one eyelid, hoping that Cathy wouldn't be coming in to comfort me for my distinct lack of visitors. Trick smiled at me and I instantly flew into his arms, breathing in every smell and trying to burn it onto my unreliable memory.

"Hey Tink. How are you doing?" He didn't let me go and I clung to him tightly in case he was a hallucination.

"Things are better now you're here." I knew I should be furious with him for sleeping with that girl but I had been so frightened that I'd have to spend the day alone that I just couldn't bring myself to push him away.

"Is this because you thought I slept with someone?" My chest tightened, not wanting him to bring it up and annoyed that he was now trying to deny it after he had already admitted it.

"Stop trying to twist things. You already told me you did it." I pulled away from him suddenly and instantly my body felt the emptiness the distance between us caused.

He frowned. “Like fuck I did. I was trying to understand how you’d got to that conclusion and then you hung up on me. I didn’t sleep with anyone Tink, I swear I didn’t.” He reached for my hand but I tugged it out of reach, suspicious of him.

“You were still with her when I called you!” I spat the words out far too loudly and I knew I’d have to be careful not to attract the attention of any of the staff.

He shook his head furiously. “No Tink. I wasn’t. I wouldn’t do that to you. I was in the studio with a band I’m working with.”

I sighed. “I saw the picture Trick. I saw you having sex with her.” I looked down at my hands, unable to meet his gaze as the memory of seeing him so deep inside someone else was boring heavily against my eyelids.

His mouth crinkled like he’d tasted something foul. “What picture? Help me understand Tink, please?”

I flung my hands out wildly in frustration. “Andy showed me a photo of you with her. You were fucking her right there, out in the open.”

Trick's face darkened and he muttered something under his breath before looking right into my eyes. "Tink, I don't know what he showed you, but I swear to you, it wasn't what happened. I took you home, got some sleep and then drove straight over to the studio. I can't make you believe me if you don't want to, but it's the truth. I finally had you, there's no-one else for me now." He reached for my hand again and this time I let him take it. "Please tell me that this situation didn't cause you to hurt yourself?"

I took in the sight of his grey eyes and I knew that there was nothing I could say to him to make this any better. Just like I had with Ben, I had managed to hurt Trick too and now the two most important men in my life were letting me push them away with my craziness. I would lose them both and be totally and completely alone forever. "Just go Trick." I wanted him gone as quickly as possible so the torment could be over and I could start to focus on living my life without the two of them. He bit his lip to prevent him from speaking again and nodded. Leaning forward he placed a soft kiss on my forehead.

“I love you Tink.” He allowed himself a final look back at me before he stepped out of my life forever.

Chapter Eight

In the next two weeks in the hospital, I had managed to get through eleven sessions with my assigned counsellor Rick without saying a word. I had become a master of the non-committal shrug. My heart was completely and irrevocably broken and the last thing I wanted was to be sat here in his office while he asked question after question on a seemingly relentless loop. He'd asked me a few days ago if I realised that my lack of answers was extending my stay. I didn't want to get better because I knew I would have to step out into the world and be completely alone and I'd rather just sit here and wait for death to take me so I shrugged, a lot.

As I sat down for my session today, Rick was noticeably absent. I stared at the clock and willed it to move with my mind, hoping that the seconds would tick by faster and I could go back to my room. I didn't even look at him when he eventually came into the room and sat down, bitterly disappointed that he bothered to show up.

"Hi Beth. Rick thought you might feel more comfortable with me. I'm Steve." I glanced up at him briefly but then went back to determinedly staring at the clock. I had no intention of talking to this new guy either. He stood up and opened the window widely, causing me to shiver as the cold draught came into the room. Then he reached up for the clock and took it down from the wall before flinging in casually out of the window. I frowned as he took his seat again. "Great, so now that's out of the way is there anything else you'd like to fixate on that we can throw out too?"

He smiled at me and the smallest of giggles escaped my lips that were traitorously threatening to tug up at the edges. He stubbornly refused to break eye contact with me and my lip started to tremble. All the emotions that I'd kept bricked up behind a wall in my mind were threatening to gush out of me like a fucking landslide. I tried to hold them back, my whole body fighting a raging war inside me until finally a single choked sob escaped. I took a breath and my head started to clear slightly. “What do you have against that clock?” I raised an eyebrow at him.

His eyes narrowed. “Why don’t you like time Beth?”

I shrugged and stared at him. Those few words were the most I’d said to anyone in over a week, since I’d told Trick to leave. Steve's eyes never left mine, waiting for a response. Like a cat in a staring contest, he fucking broke me. “Time never does what you want it to.”

He nodded as if he understood me completely. “What do you want it do?”

I blinked. “Stop, go faster, go slower, turn back. I dunno.” I could hear my heart pounding inside my eardrums.

“When do you want it to stop?”

I closed my eyes as my thoughts instantly went to the moment that Trick's lips touched mine and I held my breath again savouring the memory. My stomach turned over at the thought that my own brain was so unreliable that for all I knew I could have imagined the whole fucking thing. I wrapped my arms around myself tightly. "Can I ask you something?" He nodded slowly but didn't speak. "How do you know when something's real and when it's not?"

Steve tilted his head slightly. "Why does it matter to you?"

I bit my lip thoughtfully. "What if my whole fucking life is a lie that I created in my mind? There are so many things that I've done that I can't even remember and now I don't know if what I think is real even happened." I could hear my voice trembling as I spoke.

"If there was a way, would you want to remember all the things you've forgotten?"

I swallowed nervously. "Maybe not remembering is my mind's way of trying to protect me. Maybe I shouldn't want to remember those things, but I do. I want to know the truth." A tear spiked sharply against my eyeball and I watched it descend heavily onto the back of my hand.

Steve considered me for a moment before answering. "You'd do well in psychology Beth, you're very perceptive. Why don't you tell me something you can remember?"

I laced my fingers together in my lap and thought about something that was undeniably happy. "My mum used to make these amazing cookies when we were little. She'd always bring them out of the oven and put them on a cooling rack in the kitchen and Ben would lift me up so I could grab them. They were always too hot and burned the tips of my fingers but I was so happy sat on the floor with him licking the gooey chocolate off my fingers that I didn't care." I smiled at the memory and was sure that it was real; I could practically taste the cookies in my mouth.

"Where's your mum now Beth?"

I frowned. "What do you mean? She's at home."

"Where is she Beth?" I shook my head and an overwhelming feeling of anxiety washed through me. I unlaced my fingers and dug a nail deep into my palm feeling the relief flood through me from the spike of pain. "Beth?" Steve had knelt down in front of me and slowly pulled my hands apart leaving me feeling empty inside. "Where is she Beth?"

My breath caught in my throat and I felt like I was losing oxygen and on the verge of passing out but he just carried on, asking the same question over and over. My voice was barely a whisper as it came out of me. "She's dead." Steve nodded and moved his head so I'd have to look at him. My whole body was shaking with desperation to inflict pain, I needed it more than ever to block out the emotion that was coursing through me, completely unrestricted by my normally tight hold on it.

He still held my wrists firmly in his hands. "Tell me what happened Beth."

I tore my face away from his, unable to look at him any longer. “She…. the door….. I….man…. knife….blood…..” I managed to hiccup out a few words in between sobs and stared down at my palms that felt like they were soaking in my mother’s deep red blood. I couldn’t fight the urge to curl up tightly into a ball and tug at my hair, pulling it out by the root. I tried to move but Steve held me in place gently and I didn’t have the energy to push him away.

The tears came more easily now, aware that I wasn’t fighting them. “Tell me Beth.”

My eyes felt heavy and I could barely open them. I could hear the doorbell ringing in my mind like a persistent case of tinnitus. “The doorbell wouldn’t stop ringing. He was leaning on it and it just rang and rang. I ran to the top of the stairs and she was just standing there, not wanting to open the door. She turned to smile at me as she pushed down on the handle. If she hadn’t smiled at me then she would have seen it coming. As soon as the door was open he plunged the knife right into her chest and just ran away. He left her there, bleeding." I swallowed. "There was so much blood… so much blood." My face scrunched up tightly and I couldn't go any further.

"Tell me what you did then Beth."

"I went down to see her." Even spoken out loud it felt like a lie.

Steve shook his head at my deceit. "Tell me what really happened Beth."

I saw myself standing at the top of those fucking stairs and I felt so much heartbreak for the sixteen year old version of myself. "I threw myself down the stairs." As soon as I said it, I knew it was the truth beyond a shadow on any doubt. I'd felt myself push off forcefully and fly towards the stairs with absolute relief that I wouldn't wake up tomorrow and have to deal with anything. Except all I managed to do was to break my wrist and bruise a couple of ribs. I'd pushed myself over to her body and laid my head on her chest for hours until

Ben got home and found us. I took in a sharp breath and sniffed as my tears started to dry up.

"We're almost done for today but will you tell me another happy memory before you go?"

I looked down at my left wrist and something I had long forgotten came to mind. "Trick. He helped me." Despite the pain of the memory, a warm feeling flooded me as if Trick were in the room with me.

"Tell me Beth."

I looked at the long vertical scar on my wrist and realised I'd not noticed it before; I frowned trying to make sense of my thoughts. "I was sixteen. It was pouring with rain outside and Ben and I had fought. He'd told me something…. I can't remember what… he wanted to do something…." I shook my head in frustration because I knew I should be able to remember what we'd argued about but it was like the thought just kept getting further away.

"It's okay Beth. Just tell me what you do remember."

"He'd slammed the door on the way out and the kitchen drawer was open. I saw the knife and knew that I needed it; I needed the pain and the relief. I wanted it to all be over. I cut so deeply that blood was pouring out of me and I got scared. I called Trick and he came and helped me. He wrapped my wrist like I was precious to him. He…he brought me….here?" I looked up at Steve in confusion and he nodded, confirming that I was remembering correctly.

"He saved your life that day Beth."

Chapter Nine

Steve told me that I needed a few days to process everything I'd managed to regain and so I was excused from group and one to one sessions until after the weekend. I had so many unanswered questions inside me and I wanted to speak to Ben and Trick and see if I could somehow take back control of my memory. Every time I thought about them, my heart shattered at the thought that I would never see them again; that I had made their lives so unbearable and given them no choice but to keep their distance. When visiting day came around I frantically searched my room for anything that I could press against my skin to alleviate the growing ache in my chest.

There was a gentle tap on my door and I was instantly consumed by rage that anyone thought they could console me in this moment. “Fuck off!” The handle turned downwards and I flung my entire weight against the door to refuse them entry. “Seriously, I’m not fucking joking, get the fuck away from me.” I caught sight of my reflection in the window pane and realised I looked like a feral, caged animal. My hair was straggled down my face, my skin was pale and my eyes were wide and filled with fear.

“Tink? I’m not going anywhere. Let me in.” His voice was so soft and gentle and I felt it right through my soul.

“Trick?” My breathing was shallow and frantic and I was sure I was hallucinating.

The door pushed against me and as my determination to keep it closed subsided, he managed to slide me across the floor as he entered. “Oh Tink, come here.” He held his arms out to me with the most spine tinglingly sad smile on his face. I flopped against him and he lifted me over to the bed and held me firmly.

My Own Worst Enemy

As his scent took over my senses, I knew there was only one thing I needed more than anything right now. If I couldn't have the pain that I craved then I needed the pleasure, the physical contact. I'd held on to my virginity for too long and it was time to give it to the one person that ever meant anything to me. It was as if I'd become consumed by a singular need to establish some sort of connection with him, keep him close to me somehow. Every other thought left me and all I could focus on was his body. It was as if my muscles were aching for him.

I blinked up towards him and pushed my lips to his almost ravenously. His mouth parted to allow me access and as my tongue slid against his I shifted so I could straddle his hips. His growing erection pulsed against me as he gripped my hips and without any doubt, I knew I wanted him inside me more than I had ever wanted anything. I pulled away from him breathing hard and looked right into his beautiful grey eyes. "I want you Trick, please be my first. Please." My begging words came out as barely a breathless sob because my desire for him in that moment was overriding everything.

His brow crossed tightly and his eyes searched my face. “Shit Tink, you don’t remember do you?” He looked like he wanted to punch something really really hard.

I swallowed hard. “There’s a lot I don’t remember.” I tried to push my lips to his again but he pulled his face away from mine and lifted me off him. The emptiness I felt between my legs was absolute and sent chills down my spine.

His thumb slowly stroked the line of my trembling jaw. “Will you do something? For me?” His brows lifted slightly and I knew I would agree to anything he asked of me if only he'd never stop touching me. I nodded quickly. “Try and remember your first time.” The words hit me like a fucking freight train.

I was so sure five minutes ago that I’d never had sex before, how could I possibly have forgotten anything so momentous? Trick took my hand and slowly drew tiny circles across my wrist. I focused entirely on the sensation rippling through my body and a memory came to me that was so intense that I instinctively reached out and grabbed Trick's shoulder, digging my fingernails into his skin to brace myself.

I was at the hospital having my plaster taken off my wrist and Trick was with me. He wrapped his arms around me as we went back to his car and I moaned about how my skin felt strange without the cast. On the drive home, he made those tiny little circles across my wrist and it drove me wild for him. I threw myself at him when he opened my door and pulled my legs around his waist as he carried me into the house and upstairs to my bed. He was unbearably gentle with me as he slipped my clothes off and spent every second worshipping my body with his lips and his hands. My need for him was so vibrant that I could practically see it radiating from my skin as he touched me. When he finally slid deeply inside me I cried for the beauty of it, the perfection of having the only man I'd ever wanted buried inside me. He lay naked next to me afterwards and kissed me so sweetly as I fell asleep. He whispered to me endlessly how I was his and only his forever.

I blinked against the tears falling from my face now and looked at him aghast. This beautiful man in front of me was everything to me and somehow I had managed to blank out the most perfect moment of my whole existence. How could he ever want me again after that? “Do you remember now Tink?” His voice was thick and heavy with all the things he wanted to say.

I nodded. “I’m so sorry Trick, please forgive me.” I whimpered as he kissed my forehead.

“You don’t have anything to be sorry for Tink.” I knew that wasn’t true and the thought of all the other things I couldn’t remember was pulling at me with a painful ache. He’d wanted me then but had ended up with Annie so I must have done something awful to him and I had no recollection of it at all.

I pulled tighter to him so I could breathe in the scent of him and feel his heart against mine. “I don’t know what happened Trick but I want to find out. Please don't leave me."

His grip on me was almost painful now. "I will never leave you again, I promise you. I'm not giving up on us again." I closed my eyes as I knew with those words that I had done something so tragically and stupendously horrific that it had made him leave me and the thought was absolutely heart wrenching.

Chapter Ten

That night I had the most vivid dream, clearer than any other I'd had before. So real that there was no doubting it was a memory coming back to me.

It was pouring with rain, possibly the worst weather we'd had in years. Each corpulent raindrop thundered heavily against the window panes in angry defiance, determined to continue its journey unimpeded. I slung my useless umbrella to one side and made a dash for it as I leapt out of the door holding my coat over my head in the hope it would shield the worst of it. I'd not even made it three steps before the back of my trousers were completely sodden and water was soaking deeply into my pores. I ran on regardless, my trainers splashing in to huge puddles along the way making each step an ordeal as they become more cumbersome.

Finally under the awning outside Trick's house, my heart sank as I noticed not a single light was on inside. I pressed the bell with a silent prayer that he would be inside and I wouldn't have to make the journey back again. The door swung open and my breath caught at the sight of him.

His soft grey eyes took in the vision of me with a look of complete serenity, like he had finally found the reason for living. He stepped back to allow me in and was instantly fussing over me to get out of my wet clothes. He had me completely stripped naked in less than a minute and lifted me into his strong warm arms to carry me upstairs.

In the bathroom, he took such care to dry every part of my skin, each tender touch sending warm tingles across my body. He slid a comb slowly through my wet hair as he stood behind me and then wrapped a warm fluffy towel around my head. Leading me to his bedroom, he cocooned me in his luxurious duvet and rubbed his hands up and down my chrysalis until I giggled, warmth spreading to every part of me.

He leant forward and placed the softest kiss on my lips with a smile. "You are so beautiful." I purred softly at his words and he slipped inside the covers to be closer to me. My fingers quickly reached out for his flesh and pulled his body against mine. He kissed me again but with more urgency this time, a quiet desperation that screamed out how he couldn't bear to be parted from me. That nowhere would ever be close enough.

I tugged at his waist until he rolled on top of me and I felt his cock press firmly against my hip. He slid a finger down between my thighs and when he touched me he released a soft moan of pure desire. He traced my entrance lazily with his thick head and my back arched to find a way to manoeuvre him inside me. As he pushed in slowly, I gasped and sucked on his tongue almost frantically.

My Own Worst Enemy

As the pressure built inside my stomach, I began to move my hips more rapidly to increase his rhythm causing him to flash me a cheeky smile that only made him more desirable to me. As my release came, I nipped at his neck and he followed swiftly behind with a groan of his own. We both shuddered from the intensity of it and he withdrew himself slowly before curling up next up to me.

I lay there completely sated and listening to our breathing synchronise when he suddenly leapt out of bed like he'd been electrocuted. "Stay there, I'll be two seconds." I sat up and watched him fly out of the room, his tight bum cheeks flexing in the moonlight. I pulled the duvet up around my chest and waited.

He was back in a matter of moments, clutching something small in his hand and had the biggest, goofiest grin on his face. He knelt down on the floor beside and took my hand, his face full of excitement and happiness. I smiled at him and felt it throughout my whole being, I had never been as happy as I was right at this moment.

Trick took my hand in his and I couldn't help but notice that mine was tiny in comparison. "Tink?" I looked into his eyes and melted. "I love you. I have always loved you and every moment with you has been so unbelievably precious to me. You are the light of my life, the sunshine in the sky, the sugar in my coffee, the chopsticks in my Chinese, the cactus in my desert, the Tom to my Jerry, the Bonnie to my Clyde. Without you, I am nothing and I want to know that every single day for the rest of my life, you're all mine." He opened his hand and popped up the lid on the box he was holding. My mouth fell open at the sight of the beautiful diamond ring nestled inside. "Tink, I love you more than my own life. Will you marry me?"

My eyes shot open and I practically flew out of bed. I only made it two steps before the devastation took me over like a landslide and I crashed to the floor in a pool of my own tears.

Chapter Eleven

It took four days before I could even be conscious without breaking down completely. After they realised that not only was I completely inconsolable but that I also couldn't verbalise the problem in any way, they took to chemically sedating me for a few hours at a time so that I wouldn't hurt myself. On the fifth day, I managed one solitary word 'Trick.' By day nine, I had started to eat on my own again and by day fifteen, I was finally sat back in front of Steve, fully dressed but devoid of any sense of emotion. I was an empty shell. 'I am Jack's Broken Heart'.

"Beth? Tell me something. Anything you like." Steve seemed annoyingly wistful today and I wanted to punch him in his smarmy face. I shrugged. He rolled his fucking eyes. "Now now, there's no need for that. I'll sit here all night if I have to but you will speak to me."

I glared at him. "Fuck you."

He nodded and rubbed his hands together almost gleefully. "Okay good. So we're on the anger train today, just my area. Why don't you tell me where you stopped on your journey to get there?" I hated him but not as much as I hated myself.

I sucked my tongue sharply against my teeth. "How about the village of fuck you and the town of I couldn't give a shit what you say?" I crossed my arms, suddenly furious that I was sat in front of him when I could be staring at the wall in my room and contemplating how I could ever make the pain in my heart stop for one fucking second.

He laughed and raised his eyebrows. "Can't say I've ever been there. Do they do cake?"

My stomach growled treacherously at the thought of cake. Stupid stomach. "I don't want to talk today."

He tilted his head. “Why?” I shrugged. He sat back in his chair and crossed one leg over the other.

I could feel his ridiculous knowing eyes staring holes into my skin and I had to fight an urge to throw myself at him and claw them out. “No point.” I shrugged again to attempt some sort of signal that my life was now completely meaningless. Not only was I now regretting doing whatever it was that made the one man I had ever loved walk away from me but I also didn’t want to risk remembering anything else. I didn’t think I could handle whatever it was that I did to him and if I’d chosen to forget it then who was I to argue with my own mind? It clearly knew what was best for me. Smart arse mind.

“Don’t you want to leave here Beth? Your brother would love to have you home.”

I sighed. “Ben hates me. He doesn’t want me home.”

Steve frowned. “Well he calls here twice a day to see how you’re doing and always asks when he can come and take you home. That doesn't seem like the actions of someone who hates you does it?"

I matched his frown with my own. "You're lying. I saw it on his face, he doesn't want me anymore."

"What about Trick?" I shrugged. "Don't you want to go home so you can see more of him?" I shrugged again but this time it hurt. The mention of Trick's name was enough to stab me in the heart with an imaginary knife. "Don't you want to remember Beth?"

His words burnt me and I struggled for breath. I shook my head and covered my eyes with my hands. "It hurts too much."

I felt the sofa depress as he sat beside me and wrapped an arm around my shoulder. I leant in to him and cried until there were no tears left inside me at all. As if my mind knew exactly how to fuck me up, it pushed a memory to me, clearer than any I'd had before.

Things were pretty shitty. No that was an understatement of the highest proportions. Everything was fucking ruined. Ben saw my face and came and sat across from me. "How bad is it?"

I pushed the envelope across to him and he pulled out the paper inside. "Fuck. That bad?"

I couldn't even bring myself to agree with him. "How did you do?"

He grimaced and I hated him. I gritted my teeth for the inevitable. "It's not about me right now. Maybe you can appeal? After everything's that's happened, they're bound to take that into consideration."

I reached for Ben's cigarettes and lit one, not caring that smoking in the house was not something we ever did. "Ben, I got two E's and a U. What are they gonna do, add on twenty percent? I'm fucked. End of story."

He had the decency to look sheepish. I knew he was holding an envelope that had great grades in it. He always was too smart for his own good. "It's not the end of the world. It's not all about how good your grades are y'know."

I turned away from him in case I infected him with my own stupidity. "What did Trick get?"

Ben shrugged. "Dunno. Why don't you call him?"

"I can't. We're not talking right now." I stretched out my frustration from my tightly wound limbs.

Ben grunted. "Jesus. The two of you are just as bad as each other. Why can't one of you learn to back down, just once?"

My lips pursed. "I'm happy with that arrangement. As long as he's the one that backs down."

Ben shook his head at me. Trick and I spent a lot of time fighting with each other. Normally we weren't actually in disagreement; we just couldn't face admitting the other one was right. "Just call him because if you don't, I'll tell him you told me to pass on the message that you're sorry."

I threw Ben's lighter at him and it hit him in the forehead. "You wouldn't dare."

He raised his eyebrows. "Try me and see what happens. I'm sick of you two moping around every time you argue. It's boring."

I sighed heavily and grabbed my phone. "Fine. But just remember I did this for you next time you're whining on." He didn't respond, he just sat there grinning knowingly. I pressed the call button as I walked out of the room and Trick answered on the first ring.

"Hey Tink. How did you do?"

"I suck. I'm sure it's your fault. I should have been studying my books, not studying...well other things." I couldn't help but smile at the thought that all our revision sessions had basically ended up with us both being naked and sweaty.

He laughed sexily. "I dunno, I felt like I learnt a lot. Want me to come over and see what else I can learn?"

"Maybe later. I'm still wallowing in misery right now. How did you do?"

He made a 'pfft' sound. "I got an A in music." I cheered enthusiastically for him, glad that he'd succeeded in the thing that meant the most to him. "How did Ben do?"

"I hate him and his stupid brain. Why did he get the looks and the brains?"

Trick laughed at my annoyance. "Tink trust me. You did not come up short in the looks department. Anyway, it's not like you have to decide what to do right this second, why don't you just do something that's just for you for a while? Find something you love and go for it?"

I thought about it. Since our mum died and left us the house and a pretty amazing insurance policy, we didn't need to work. The problem was, I didn't have anything I was passionate about. Not like Trick with his music or Ben and his art. I liked things just fine but nothing ever took a hold of me, made me feel like it was an extension of my soul. Except for Trick and I didn't think I could make him into a career without taking a pretty abstract turn on the path of life. "Ugh, I think I'm probably destined for a name badge life baby."

"No way. You're destined for greatness. I can feel it. Now let me come over so I can feel you."

I chuckled. "Fine, but you have to pay the toll and tell my brother that he's too damn smart for his own good when you get here."

"It's a deal Tink. See you in ten."

I went back to my room with a heavy feeling in my chest. I was sure the loneliness of being without them was going to eat me alive.

Chapter Twelve

Visiting day was upon me again and this time I was filled with dread that someone might actually turn up. I didn't want to fight with Ben and I didn't want another Trick encounter to trigger more memories. I buried my head under the pillows and hoped no-one would notice me. It didn't work. Trick's hand stroked my back gently and I heard him chuckle softly.

"I know your body like the back of my own hand Tink. You're not asleep. Turn around please."

I screamed into the pillow. "Just go away. I don't want to see you."

"Well I want to see you so I guess you're stuck with me. It would be much easier for you to breathe properly if you turned round though." Stupid man, why couldn't he just leave me alone?

"I think that's highly unlikely. Just go. Please?" I sobbed once and he shifted so he could massage my shoulders. I involuntarily groaned in pleasure and shrugged him off, annoyed with my body for giving me away.

"No way. I promised you, I'm not giving up this time. You can't push me away. Now either turn around and talk to me or I'm coming in to get you."

I shook my head violently. Undeterred he whipped the pillows out from around my head and threw them on to the floor as my head hit the mattress with a thump. I tried to squirm further away but he held me firmly, flipped me over and quickly positioned himself around my waist, straddling my hips. His full weight wasn't on me but he was still much stronger than I was. I hit out with my fists but he easily clamped both my wrists securely in one hand and then used the other to turn my head to face him. I relented slightly as I looked into his beautiful grey eyes and stopped fighting, instead overcome with grief and despair.

"Talk to me Tink. What's going on with you? Why don't you want to see me?"

I caught sight of my hands bundled up inside his and my ring finger suddenly felt empty and deserted. "Where's my ring?" I barely murmured but he definitely heard it, lifting my hands to his lips so he could place a tiny kiss where my ring had been.

"I'll bring it next time if you still want it. Or I'll get you a new one. Whatever you want Tink." His eyes were rimmed red now and I felt the sincerity in what he said.

"I want my one. Is that okay?" I didn't want just any ring; I wanted the one that he gave me when he surrendered his heart to me. Even if it was the same one he took back when I stomped all over his heart and pushed him towards Annie.

A smile crept painfully slowly across his face. "Of course it is, of course it is. I'll bring next time, I promise." He touched the back of my hand against his cheek and closed his eyes. "I'm so happy you remember Tink. I love you so much." Trick sighed contentedly as I took in an anguished breath, full of the pain I'd caused him.

"I…. I don't want….I can't…. I hurt you… I don't know what I did." I scrunched my eyes tight to try and stop the tears from falling because I didn't feel like I deserved to be the one in pain for what I did to him.

He licked his lips slowly and looked at me. "It doesn't matter Tink, none of that matters now. I love you so much and I just want you to start feeling better. Please just focus on getting well baby, that's all that matters." He leaned down and our lips touched, his tears falling onto my skin.

"Things are better when you're here."

He grimaced and looked away before answering. "I wish that were true Tink. I wish I knew how to help you." He looked like he wanted to say more and for a split second I actually thought someone was going to tell me something without me having to be cornered into recalling it. I couldn't tell if I was delighted, excited or petrified. Trick just shook his head. “Ben’s here, if I let you up will you see him?”

“I can’t see him. I don’t want to disappoint him again, he already hates me enough as it is.”

Anger flashed across Trick’s face. “Who the fuck told you that? Ben could never hate you babe, he fucking loves the life out of you. He misses you. I miss you. We’re just so fucking worried about you Tink.”

I shook my head. “No, you’re wrong. I saw him. He was so sad, so empty. I destroyed him. He hates me.” I whimpered and tried to turn away but Trick held me firmly in place.

He closed his eyes with a sigh and I saw him mouthing the numbers as he counted to ten. When he’d finished, he turned ever so slowly to face me. “I love you. Ben loves you. We don’t hate you and we never, NEVER, will. Whatever else you want to twist in your mind, whatever you want to forget or push or corrupt, don’t ever think for one second that we won’t be here for you Tink. We love you. Now give us some fucking credit and start working on getting better."

He started to lift off me and the feeling of desertion crept through me. I knew if I didn't say something now then everything I had ever wanted would be walking right out of the door. As he released my wrists, I put one down on his thigh softly, still giving him the option of pushing me away. "Trick?" He stopped moving and was completely still. "I'm sorry."

I meant every syllable and I meant it for everything that I couldn't remember as well as those things I could. He nodded and bent to kiss my forehead. "I know Tink, I know." He walked away without another word.

I felt too raw and open when Ben came in. My emotions were scattered carelessly around the room and I didn't know how to go about putting them all back in the right place. He smiled his sweet easy-going smile and the tears fell from my eyes far too easily. When he held my hand, I actually felt like I was going to die right there in front of him. There were no words to say what I needed to, to beg him to still love me, to fall down on my knees in front of him and hope that he could forgive me for doing this to him.

"You look tired B. I won't stay long; I just wanted to say hi." He stuck his tongue out at me like he used to do when we were little and I felt my eyes getting heavy. I blinked a few times but each time, my lids stayed closed for a little longer. He stroked my cheek and shushed me gently, his smile still focused entirely on me. I didn't hear him leave, but when I woke up, he was gone.

Chapter Thirteen

I leant forward intently in my chair, my hands clasped in front of me. “Okay, here’s the situation.” Steve raised an eyebrow but didn’t comment. “I want to get out of here and I don’t want to hurt the people I care about anymore. But. I don’t want to have to remember anything else. Can you help me?” I’d been planning what to say over and over for two days and hoped that he would have enough faith in me to believe it was the truth. I didn’t have anything else to give.

Steve ran his tongue over his teeth distractedly before he answered. “You do realise you’re not on a hold right?”

I frowned. No, I didn’t know that, but then I had been pretty out of it and not focused on what was happening. “So I can just leave? Whenever I want to?” I sounded as unsure as I felt.

Steve nodded. “If you want to, yes. Is that what you want Beth?”

“What if I hurt myself again?” I looked down at my wrists and was shocked to see how many scars were there. I silently started counting and then decided against it once I got past fifteen.

Steve sat back in his chair and looked at me. “I don’t think you will. Do you?”

His confidence confused me and sent my mind spinning. “I don’t know.”

“Yes you do. Do you know how many times you’ve been here Beth?” I shrugged and shook my head. “Seven. Seven times you’ve been admitted here and this is the first time you’ve remembered anything. I know you’re getting better. You just have to believe it yourself now.”

Wow. Seven times. I knew I’d been here before somehow, I knew the name and some things were recognisable to me. I had muscle memory for the height of the bed and I knew my way around without getting lost. The curtains were seared into my mind probably because of the horrid yellow pukey colour they were. Those things were so tangible but yet I had no actual memory of being here. “Will I ever remember it all?” Please say no, please say no, please say no, please say no, please say no, please say no, please say no, please say no.

“Maybe. If you let yourself heal, it will come back in time. If you fight it, then it won’t. But ask yourself why don’t you want to remember? Even the most painful things are tempered by the most beautiful ones. You would be missing out on an awful lot of special things just so you didn’t have to experience the traumatic things. And those things make us who we are Beth. Without suffering there would be no compassion. Without heartbreak, there would be no love. Let it in Beth before you wake up one day and realise that everything you could have had in your life has passed you by."

I sniggered uncomfortably. "Wow. That shit just got deep man." He grinned at my sarcasm. "Can I leave today?"

He nodded once. "If you want to. I'd rather you stayed for a while, tried to work through some of your missing memories with me. I could really help you, if you'll let me?"

"I want you to help me, but I want to go home more. I need to go home." Being able to see Trick every day and being at home in my own bed were top priorities for me right now. The memories would come or they wouldn't but I couldn't stay here a moment longer if I didn't have to.

"How about you come and see me as an outpatient? We could meet once a week and you could bring someone with you if you wanted? I'd really like to help you Beth."

I agreed but I was unsure if it was because I wanted to get out of that room as fast as humanly possible or if it was because I really did want him to help me. All I could think about in that moment was getting home and back in my own bed with Trick's ring on my finger. I needed him to know that I was his before he left me again.

Chapter Fourteen

Steve had advised me that I should really get someone to collect me but I didn't want that. I needed to go back on my own terms so I called a taxi and nervously played with my sleeve for the entire journey. I gave him Trick's address because I couldn't bring myself to just turn up on my brother just yet. I needed to have a conversation first and for all I knew I'd end up right back in Risemoor at the end of it. I rang the bell and stood waiting impatiently, concentrating on my breathing and on not freaking out.

He opened the door and just stood perfectly still, staring at me. A frown crossed his face and then he ushered me further outside, closing the door to behind him. "Tink? What are you doing here?" He didn't seem at all pleased to see me and was edging towards annoyed.

"I didn't break out or anything if that's what you're thinking." I folded my arms, upset with him for not instantly embracing me. I suddenly felt stupid and pathetic that I'd let myself believe this beautiful man could ever love me.

He scratched his nose, the frown still in place. "That's not what I was thinking. Why didn't you call? We could have come and picked you up."

I scowled at him, fury building inside the pit of my stomach. "Sorry to inconvenience you." I turned on my heel and started to storm away like a stroppy teenager. I hated that I couldn't even walk away from him properly.

He jogged alongside me, keeping pace with me. "Stop Tink. Come back please."

I stared resolutely ahead and kept walking, trying to quicken my pace but unable to match his lengthy strides. Stupid tall stupid sexy man.

He jogged ahead of me and put his hands on my arms, holding me still. "Stop Tink." I tried to wriggle free but he had me too tight. “What the fuck is going on? Are you mad at me?”

I sighed. “Yes.”

His lips twitched up in a smirk and I wanted to kick him in the leg. But I didn’t. “Why?”

“Why aren’t you happy to see me?” God, even I could hear how sulky and pathetic I was sounding.

He chewed on his lip for a moment and assessed me with his eyes. I felt like my insides were going to turn outside in the rush to display themselves for him. “You dozy bird. I fucking LOVE you. When are you ever gonna understand that? You turn up at my place and all I can think is how I haven’t cleaned in about three weeks and you’re gonna leave me as soon as you see it. I’m thinking how I can get you naked in my bed without you having to open your eyes or breathe in. I’m thinking that I haven’t had a shower since Saturday because I can still smell you on my fucking skin and I daren’t wash it away. I’m thinking that my dreams have all come true and if I say anything else you’re going to walk away from me again and I will have to fall down right here and die. I fucking love you. Love you. When are you gonna get that?"

His eyes caught mine right before he crushed his mouth against mine and as he slipped his tongue inside me, my knees trembled and I had to lean against him for support. Trick held me effortlessly as he ravaged me in the street and when he finally pulled away, we were both panting like we'd run a marathon. I could barely focus on his features as my vision blurred. He tossed his arm around my neck and walked next to me back to his house.

Trick wasn't lying; the place was a complete shit tip. Empty takeaway boxes were strewn everywhere and there was a distinctive dirty boy smell about the place. My nose crinkled involuntarily and I had to suppress the urge to vomit in my mouth. He chuckled at my reaction with an air of 'I told you so'. Taking my hand, he pulled me upstairs. "Come on Tink, I've got something for you."

He took the stairs two at a time and I struggled to keep pace with him. Going in to his room, I realised the only memory I had of ever being in here had been within the dream I'd had. I looked around and examined everything, trying to get my bearings. As I plopped down on the bed, the mattress seemed to rise up slightly to greet me and I felt immensely welcome and at home, like this was where I should have been all along. A thought struck me as he was rummaging in his drawers and it was out of my mouth before I instantly regretted it. "Is this the same bed you had when you were with Annie?"

Trick's shoulders visibly tensed as he turned to face me with a look of absolute horror and anguish. I inwardly cringed at my complete stupidity and lack of any compassion. "Tink....." His mouth opened a few more times but no sound came out.

I jumped up and threw my arms around him. "Shit babe, I'm sorry. I didn't mean that."

He held me out at arm's length and studied me before smashing his fist against the top of his drawers sharply. “Fuck!” He turned away for a second and I stood there unable to move for fear of upsetting him any further. When he turned back, he seemed a lot calmer. “Here.” He shoved a tiny black box into my hands and I stared at it in disbelief. I flipped the lid and exhaled when I took in the sight of the beautiful engagement ring. “Will you wear it?” He stared intently until I nodded and then the tiniest of smiles twitched on his lips.

He slid it easily on to my finger and I was deluged with a slew of warm emotions. It felt perfectly right on my finger as if it had never been off. I clutched my hand to my chest in case it tried to escape. “I need you to tell me what happened Trick. Please?” I knew I had to know before this went any further.

He shook his head and swallowed tensely. “I can’t tell you Tink, I’m not allowed. Ben would kick my ass if I did.”

I frowned. “Why?”

“Because all the counsellors you’ve had have all said that you need to want to remember and do it on your own. You'd never accept it as the truth until you get there on your own. I want to tell you everything Tink, believe me I do. If I could, then I would."

I did believe him but I had to know. As much as I didn't want to remember the look of pain on his face when I did whatever I did, if we were really going to make this as serious as we both seemed to want then I needed to be a co-conspirator, not a consequential witness. "Will you help me then? Give me signposts at least so I can follow them?"

He frowned for a moment trying to understand my request and then his eyebrows shot up. "Wait here, I think I have something." He ran out of the room and I sat back down on the bed, unable to resist the urge to lift his pillow to my face and inhale the scent of him. When he came back, he held out something to me so proudly that I couldn't help but smile at him.

I took it and turned it over in my hands. It was a perfectly smooth dark green pebble. I ran it between my fingers, feeling the weight and the texture. There was not a single imperfection on the immaculately weather worn surface and the green colour was deep like the ocean but bright like the sun. My lips parted slightly as the memory started to flood in.

It was too hot. Definitely too hot for the seaside but he'd made me go anyway. The whole journey I'd been a crabby bitch, whining about not having the right flip flops and being devoid of an ample supply of water. My skin had stuck to the leather seats in his car and I could feel sweat rolling down my back in waves. My skin felt red and overheated and all I wanted to do was take a shower and curl up next to a fan. Trick had refused to be drawn into the fight I was seemingly determined to pick with him, staring resolutely at the road the whole way. When we finally arrived, I slammed the door shut behind me and stormed away from him, prepared to play out my tantrum at any cost. By the time I'd crossed the car park and was heading out on to the main street, I realised I couldn't feel him by my side and swung round to check he was at least following along behind. He was a good few steps back and smirked at me as I turned. Irritating man.

I turned into the high street and could hear my stomping footsteps gaining momentum as I threw everything I had into each one. I felt ridiculously over dramatic but I didn't care. I wanted him to know that I was angry with him for bringing me here. As I carried on, the air became thick with the smell of the sea. The salty freshness filled my lungs and overpowered my senses and as I reached the end of the road I was physically stopped in my tracks by the beauty of what was in front of me. It was a beautiful vast deep blue that seemed to stretch on for miles, lazily rolling back towards the coast.

Trick's arm slipped around my waist. "It's not as beautiful as you Tink." I forgot that I was mad at him and rested my head against his chest while we stood and watched the slow ebb and flow of the water. There were other people everywhere on the beach below but in that moment; it felt like we were the only two people in the whole world. "Last one in's a douchebag." His arm was pulled away suddenly as he sprinted towards the sea.

I squealed at his cheekiness and ran after him. In a moment of wanton abandon, in utter disregard for everyone else around and with a desire to win, I called his name. As he turned round to smirk at me, I pulled my dress right over my head and dropped it on to the sand. He stopped still and his mouth fell open as I ran past him and right into the freezing water. I screamed as my skin made contact, Trick finally collecting himself and grabbing me up in his arms. He smiled mischievously before dropping me right into the water. I managed to hook my fingers around his jeans and pull him right down with me. Once we were both completely drenched, Trick took off his t-shirt and covered me up with it before we went in search of my dress.

The amount of female attention he got with his shirt off did not go unnoticed and as soon as I had my dress back on I insisted he put his shirt back on immediately.

Being soaking wet, it did nothing to alleviate the stares he got as it clung to every muscle like some twisted soft porn fantasy. He held my hand tightly with a chuckle as he saw them drooling over him. "Don't worry about it Tink, there's only one woman for me."

"That better be me you're talking about." I put my free hand on my hip in a display of mock disgust.

He bent down and held out a shiny green pebble to me. "Look at this." I took it and stared down at it. "It's as deep as the ocean and as bright as the sun, perfectly smooth and when you have it in your hand, you could never imagine letting go. It's just like you Tink."

My heart melted at his words and I let him sweep me into his strong arms for the most wonderfully passionate kiss in the world.

I blinked. "I remember this." He smiled with a small sigh. "I love you Trick. I'm sorry I hurt you."

"Don't worry about it Tink, it's all in the past now. You're here now and that's all that matters." He sat down next to me and held me close to him. I still couldn't shake the feeling that whatever I'd done was truly awful and that at any moment, this was all going to come crashing down around us.

Chapter Fifteen

Ben was nervous around me as I sat on the sofa clutching Trick's hand like it was the only thing keeping me grounded. He paced for a while asking an endless stream of questions that took Trick warning him off gently before he relented and sat down himself. His leg bounced with unreleased energy and his eyes couldn't seem to focus on a single point for more than a millisecond. He made me exhausted just watching him and I was soon curled up in Trick's lap while he stroked my hair and softly soothed me to sleep.

When I woke up, they were talking quietly and I took the opportunity to wickedly eavesdrop, not opening my eyes and feigning unconsciousness.

"You can't tell her man. I mean it. She has to find out for herself."

My Own Worst Enemy

"Fuck Ben, you're killing me here. She still thinks there was something between me and Annie. I can't keep lying to her. She's going to start asking questions I don't have the answers to."

"Trick, please? Do you really want things to go back to how they were before when she'd cut herself and not even acknowledge it had happened?"

"Of course I don't. Jesus, how many times did I find her like that? Those days nearly tore me apart. But I love her. I need her to know how I feel about her. There can't be any doubt in her mind that she's the only one for me. I can't live like that."

"She's already remembering more than I ever thought possible. Just give it a few weeks at least, let her settle in a bit and see if things start coming back. Does she remember what happened when Annie died?"

"She's still here isn't she? I've only seen her remember happy things, I don't know if she could cope with something as bad as that. Does she remember your mum?"

"Yeah. Steve said that was pretty early on. He doesn't know what sent her spiralling though. I just want to protect her; I wish I could make it easier, less painful."

"You are preaching to the choir brother. I'd move her in with me right now if I didn't think it would make her worse."

"Yeah, we don't want a repeat of last time. You should probably stay here for a few days though, let her get used to having you around. If you've got no work on then I know I'd feel better if you were here with her in the day."

"I moved a few things around as soon as she turned up on my doorstep. I'll be here as long as she wants me."

"You mean until she remembers?"

Trick sighed. "Am I a fucking monster for hoping there are some things she never gets back?"

"No, I was just thinking the same thing."

I heard Ben get up and leave, indistinct noises emanating from the kitchen. I felt like a traitor for listening to their conversation and I couldn't shake the feeling that I should sit straight up and demand they tell me everything. I wanted to know what they meant when they spoke about Annie. I needed to know. I forced myself back inside my own mind to look for anything I could remember about her.

"Hey bitches. What's going on?" Annie slipped in between me and Georgie, swinging an arm round each of us.

"Not much. Just hanging out I guess." Georgie had always felt intimidated by Annie's presence, as if at any moment her insignificance as a human being would be displayed for all to see. I on the other hand, harboured a deeply entrenched loathing for the girl because she wanted the one thing that meant anything to me.

"Okay cool. So B, where's your boyfriend today?" She said 'boyfriend' with utter derision in her tone.

I shrugged. "He's out somewhere. Where's yours?" I couldn't resist a dig at the fact that she was alone.

She flicked my ear with her hand. "Cheeky monkey! You'll soon by crying into your sarcastic face when Trick finally realises he's wasting time with a loser like you and comes to see what a real woman feels like."

I shuddered, unable to remove the mental image of her hands all over Trick's body. "Fuck off Annie. Why don't you go and bug someone who actually gives a shit."

She removed her arms and flicked back her long blonde hair. Not only did she love Trick but she was also far more beautiful than I was and far closer to his type. My brother had done all her tattoos and they made her appear edgy and interesting. He'd taken his time just like always and finished them to such a high standard that I knew at least one of them was in his portfolio. He'd done a perfect job on mine too but hers made her seem cool and natural while mine just made me feel every inch of the fraud I saw when I looked in the mirror. I knew Trick had seen the ones on her arms and looked at them with genuine appreciation. I trusted him, he'd never given me any reason not to, but I didn't trust her.

I hated the way she was around him. They liked the same music and talked about things that I would never understand. They both knew about obscure punk bands and rare imported B-sides. She was almost as musically gifted as Trick and I'd watched them discuss timbre and pitch like it was Coronation Street. As Ben had once pointed out to me, I couldn't even tell if one of the speakers was broken and had no low end, whatever the fuck that meant.

"You know girls; you two really need to get laid. You're always so uptight. Now, just point me in the direction of that sexy fine ass man and I'll be out of your hair." She jumped down in front of us and craned her neck like we'd somehow managed to position Trick just out of her line of sight.

I sighed and stood up to come level with her. "Look Annie, he's not here. Just go home please?"

She pursed her lips tightly and scowled at me. "Okay then, I'll go. Just give him a message from me?" I raised an eyebrow as confirmation although I had absolutely no intention of doing any such thing. "Tell him I said that I like his new tattoo." She smirked wickedly and stalked away.

I almost fell back against the wall we'd been sitting on as if the air had been sucked right out of my chest. Georgie dropped her head down closely to me. "B? Has Trick got a new tattoo?"

I nodded. "Yes. On his fucking arse." I didn't want to doubt him but I couldn't help it. There was no way she could know about it without having seen it. Trick took his body very seriously and was always reluctant to tell anyone what his ink meant to him or show it off proudly. It was too personal to him. Ben had done it and he was the most secretive little squirrel in the whole gang so she wouldn't have heard it from him either. I wanted to believe that she was just doing it to get a rise out of me, dropping the bait and hoping I'd scurry towards it so she could release the trap.

The thoughts stayed with me all day and when Trick didn't answer his phone, they became unbearable. I started imagining him with her, kissing her neck while he undid her bra. Pulling her nipples into his mouth and sliding his hand between her thighs. I could see the look of smug satisfaction spread out across her face as he laid her down and entered her with his hard cock and it made me want to rip her stupid blonde extensions right out of her head.

The images swirled round in my mind making a blurry Trick and Annie shaped kaleidoscope as I slid the knife out of the drawer and held the blade flat to my skin. They laughed and kissed as the edge snagged on my flesh and pushed down harder. As the blood started to drip from my arm onto the kitchen tiles, all I could see was him coming inside her with a ferocious roar.

Then Trick was there, standing beside me crying and saying things I couldn't understand as the edges of my vision blurred. There was blood all over his shirt and his heart was pounding heavily as he held me. I screamed as I.....

I sat up straight and far too suddenly and screamed. Trick held me firmly and got in my line of sight as Ben practically scrambled back in to the room. "Tink? Talk to me baby. What's going on?"

"Annie." I was all I could manage as he exhaled and pulled me closer to him, stroking my back.

I felt him tilt his head in Ben's direction and his deep voice reverberated in his chest against my cheek. "I told you this was a bad fucking idea man." I didn't hear the response as I concentrated on breathing before I passed out completely.

Chapter Sixteen

After two days with no new memories, I was starting to get angsty. I felt like a ticking bomb with no timer, never really sure when it would go off. Trick was on edge around me all the time, constantly offering to get me a drink or a blanket or something to eat or anything. I wanted to read it as sweet and caring but I couldn't stop hating him a little bit for not instantly defying my brother and telling me everything.

In addition to my foul and storm clouded mood, I had begun to notice things about my body that I'd not seen before. The scars on my wrists were not only plentiful but actually really ugly. There was no uniformity to them and they crisscrossed at strange angles in deep thick pink and silver lines. My thighs were worse; each scar was oddly shaped and angry. There was a single long scar across my stomach that had jagged edges. I traced its line with my fingertips and couldn't even imagine how I'd done it. I called Trick from the bathroom and stood in front of him completely naked. He smiled sweetly at me, his eyes burning with obvious desire for me. I had no concept of how he could look at my scarred and damaged body and feel anything but repulsion but yet here he was in front of me already semi-erect and seemingly ready to devour me.

"I know you won't tell me anything but will you at least give me yes or no answers?" I put my hands on my hips and waited.

He seemed to think about it for a long time before he answered. "Okay, I can do that." He watched me suspiciously, aware that I might be trying to trap him into saying something he shouldn't.

I stroked the scar on my stomach again. "Did I do this to myself?" I don't know why I asked but it just seemed too different to my other scars.

He held my gaze firmly as he answered, almost willing me on to the truth. “No.”

“Did you do it?”

His eyebrows raised. “No.” He seemed disgusted at the idea that I would even think such a thing.

I exhaled; pleased that I hadn’t just uncovered something I’d been silently dreading. “Did you see it happen?”

His brow tightened. “Yes.” The word was strained as it left his lips, the memory almost too much for him to recall.

I let my fingers slide over the damaged skin and felt an urge to cup my stomach protectively. As I cupped my hand against my skin, my thumb stroked against me lightly in a wave. There was something there, hidden in my mind and I knew I had to find a way to unlock it. There had to be a key, I just needed the right question to open it. I looked up at Trick to see if his face would guide me to the answer and I saw his eyelashes were heavy with tears. “This hurt you too?”

"Yes." He sniffed and I knew I was missing something. I took a few steps until I was standing in front of him and he instinctively placed his hand on my stomach in his grief. That was enough to snap the memory right into my mind like an evil hurricane.

Trick's hand was on my stomach like a protective blanket. "I'm sorry; I don't think I'll ever be able to stop this. I might have to learn to eat one handed."

I giggled at him. "What about in the shower or when you play guitar?"

He shook his head. "I'll find a way to do it with just one hand. Anything so I don't have to stop doing this. I love you so much Tink."

Trick bent down and kissed me softly on the lips. "Come on you ridiculous man. Get me something to eat before I eat you."

He licked his lips seductively. "Well I don't have a problem with that but I think I know someone who might." He squeezed my stomach gently. "Come on then, let me get my baby mama some dinner."

I smiled at his terrible attempt at an American accent and pushed the door of the nearest café open. The warmth and smells hit me immediately making my face flush. Trick eyed me with concern. "I'm okay, I just need to eat." He nodded grimly and sat me down before signalling for the waitress to attend to us immediately.

She came to take our order, her eyes roving approvingly across Trick's muscular biceps although he only had eyes for me. He ordered two plain ham sandwiches, knowing that pretty much everything else made me nauseous. "I love you Tink. Today has been the greatest day of my life." He reached out for my hand and squeezed it tightly.

I thought back to how his face had lit up when the sound of the steady heartbeat of our baby had filled the room and he'd fixated on the tiny grey blob on the screen. I never thought that I could ever feel as utterly content as I did in those moments, watching him see the new life we'd created together. Even after eight years, the love I felt for him was unrelenting. "I love you too Trick." I shoved the sandwich in my mouth and chewed. He watched me eat intently, pleased that something was actually going in after a good few weeks of me not being able to be around any type of food at all. "What do you want to do this afternoon then? I don't have to work until tomorrow."

He grinned wickedly at me. "I have a few ideas and they all involve you being naked." He raised an eyebrow and his eyes flicked down to my cleavage. My heart began to speed up slightly at the thought of being able to show him how much he meant to me, pulling him close to me as we made love.

I was so focussed on my dirty thoughts as he smiled at me that I barely noticed Annie come in and sit down next to me. It was only when Trick sat up straighter and frowned that I even thought to follow his eye line.

My Own Worst Enemy

"Hi bitch. I hear you're having a baby with MY man." She practically snarled at me and I could barely register her words.

Trick had started to stand up, to manoeuvre her away from me but he was too late. By the time he had hold of her, she had already plunged the knife into my stomach with a triumphant roar.

Tears were no longer pouring out of me, my eyeballs had all but dissolved and there was just a torrent of water sloshing out of my face. I fell to my knees as my whole world faded to black.

Chapter Seventeen

There was a familiar numbness inside me that made me nervous. I could feel the cloak of repression threatening to curl across my mind and I struggled to push it back. I didn't want to forget anything, not this time. I wanted the pain inside me to remind me of how I had destroyed Trick's world when I lay on the floor in that café losing our baby. I needed it so that I would forever know how truly grateful I was that he could even bear to look in my direction again. He had trusted me to look after the one thing that meant everything to him and I had failed. I had no idea how he managed to sit so calmly, comforting my pathetic sobs without visibly recoiling from the contact and vomiting all over my treacherous face. I was beyond redeemable and I didn't deserve his love.

My Own Worst Enemy

I had no idea how long he'd held me for but I knew that I had to say something. There had to be some words inside my head that would somehow make him understand how inexplicable it was to me that he was even here with me right now and that I didn't want him to leave. I hated that I was so selfish and that I was prepared to have him suffer alongside me instead of moving on with his life with someone who hadn't destroyed him but I didn't care. Trick Travers was the only man for me and if he was willing to stay then I wasn't going to push him away now.

I looked up at him and he smiled so sweetly that I nearly didn't say anything at all. "I know you said you couldn't but I need you to help me Trick. I need to know the rest and I can't keep reliving it, it's just too painful. Please Trick." I pleaded with him with my whole body and hoped he would take pity on me, even though it was the last thing I deserved. I glanced down at the symbol of his commitment to me while he considered my demand silently.

His heartbeat was solid and steady as I rested against his chest, waiting for any sort of response. His sigh was so pregnant with frustration and concern that I almost took back everything I'd asked. "I'll tell you anything you want to know Tink, but only if Steve says it's okay first." He squeezed me tighter, confirming his insistence on his decision.

I really didn't want to have to ask permission to talk to my own fiancé but I knew that Trick was coming from a place of care and love. I nodded sullenly and pulled my phone out of my pocket. If this was going to happen, I needed it to happen now before my mind started having ideas of its own and hid things that had already come back. I pressed the call button, not taking my eyes from Trick's.

They put me through almost immediately once I declared myself so I presumed that Steve had warned them that I might be in touch. He seemed pleased to hear from me, although slightly surprised. "I'm remembering things more clearly now but there's so much still missing. Trick agreed to help fill me in on some things but only if you say it's okay. Is it okay?" I spoke quickly and firmly, not wanting him to think that I was concerned about what might happen.

He cleared his throat. "I wouldn't recommend it Beth. Your mind is very fragile right now and if it can't reconcile what you believe with the truth that someone tells you then there's a risk it could shut down to protect you. You could end up losing all the progress you've already made. Is there something in particular you are concerned about not knowing?"

This was what not what I wanted him to say and I grimaced as Trick's brows knitted tightly. "Yes there is. I'm not sure I ever really knew it at all though, it feels like I'd started to shut down as it was happening and I don't think there's anything there to remember." I knew that I was on to something. The events after Annie stabbed me weren't there, I could feel that. Only my imagined reality remained and if that were true then I would never know what happened unless someone told me.

“That makes sense. You have been building up quite a house of cards around what you wanted to believe for quite some time. When it first started, you would have shut out anything that didn’t fit. If that’s all you want to know then I say let him tell you. Just please be careful Beth. Don’t try to take too much in at once. Take each piece of information and fit it carefully into the bigger picture like a jigsaw. Try to stick to facts, not feelings and the rest will come with time. How does that sound?”

“Will you talk to Trick and tell him what he needs to do please? I don’t know how to explain that.” I raised an eyebrow in question and Trick nodded enthusiastically.

“Of course, put him on the phone.” I handed it over and went into the kitchen. I didn’t want to have to listen to the rules and the instructions and I had absolute faith that Trick would take it seriously and do what had to be done.

I reached into the bread bin for Ben's secret cigarette stash and took the box and lighter outside into the garden. I couldn't remember the last time I'd smoked but I figured it could have as easily have been yesterday as ten years ago. As I lit up and took a drag, the nicotine rushing into my blood stream, I was slightly alarmed to realise it probably wasn't all that long ago. Trick came out to join me as I was stubbing out the end against the brickwork. He lit up and settled himself in the chair next to me, his foot resting casually on the seat of another. As he exhaled a thick cloud of smoke, his grey eyes watched me.

"Are you sure about this Tink? What if it changes things for you?"

I frowned. "I don't think it will change how I feel about you if that's what you mean." I touched my ring with the pad of my thumb, feeling angry with myself for putting him in this position.

"We'll see I guess." He rolled his cigarette around in his fingertips, fixated on the way the smoke twisted in varied directions.

"What happened after Annie stabbed me?" It was blunt I knew but I had to have answers, even it meant making Trick have to go through it all with me.

He inhaled sharply and pursed his lips. "I'd never seen so much blood in my whole life. You were there, opposite me, glowing with life and happiness and then you were crumpled on the floor and covered in blood. I thought that my life was over. I'd just watched her take everything from me and it was like the Earth stopped turning. Everything went into super slow motion. The rage consumed me and I just reached out for her and grabbed her throat and threw her right through the window. I didn't think about what I was doing, I just wanted her far away from you. I bent down to pick you up in my arms and held you until the ambulance came." His eyes flicked to mine, waiting for my judgement but I had none. I loved him for the way his instinct was to protect me at all costs.

I reached out and squeezed his hand. “I’m okay Trick. Please keep going.” I knew this was hard for him but I needed to hear it.

“I went with you to the hospital and had to wait for ages while they helped you. Ben came and sat beside me and we both just stared at the wall, too scared to move in case they came back with news. When they told us you were in recovery I was desperate to see you so I could check for myself that you were still alive. I didn’t even register at first when they told me the baby had died. Ben had to tell me. Then I just wanted to get to you so I could hold your hand and make sure you weren’t heart broken. I needed to tell you that everything was going to be alright.”

I felt terribly guilty about his concern for me and wanted to tell him how sorry I was for what I’d done to him but I needed him to continue. “I love you Trick. Please carry on.”

He slipped another cigarette between his lips and his hands shook as he lit it. He was visibly pale now and I knew that whatever he was about to say was the worst part. "I went into your room and you smiled at me but then looked right past me at Ben. I came and sat on the bed next to you and leant in to kiss you but you pulled away with a strange look on your face. It was like you barely knew me. You seemed embarrassed when I held your hand, uncomfortable with me. I was a fucking mess Tink. I didn't know what to think, it was like everything that had happened had been some weird dream. Ben made me wait outside while he spoke to you and it felt like my fucking heart was being ripped out. He was a white as a sheet when he came out and just kept going on about needing to find a doctor. We were waiting while you were examined when the police came and arrested me. Annie had been pronounced dead on the scene and they had twenty witnesses who saw me throw her through the fucking window."

He ran his hand through his hair as he took another shaky drag on his cigarette. I had no words for him; I couldn't comprehend how it all could have happened so suddenly. I had forgotten him; I had forgotten us in barely an instant.

"Ben came to see me when I was on remand and explained everything to me. How you'd repressed your memory and created an alternative version. I was completely dead inside by then, I thought I'd lost you forever. I had a supervised release to go to our baby's funeral and I spent every day beforehand praying that you'd see me and remember everything. When I got there Ben told me you thought we were at Annie's funeral and that you thought I was upset because I'd been in love with her when she died. I tried to tell you how I felt about you, I tried to tell you that I'd come back for you but you just smiled at me like I'd gone crazy. Every time Ben came to visit me, I had to keep asking him if it was real, the way you were with me made me think I was the one who had dreamt the whole thing. I got four years for manslaughter but I only served eighteen months."

"When I came out, my only option was to start again, rebuild my life and hope that one day you'd come back to me. When I felt strong enough to handle it, I started to ease myself back in to your life and thought maybe I could make you fall in love with me again. Ben wasn't happy about it; he thought I might end up driving you over the edge if I couldn't keep the past from you. I had to be so careful around you and some days it was the hardest thing I've ever had to do. It was so easy to tell you I loved you, to slip back into our routines and I had to force myself to keep my distance, take things slow. When you started to remember me, it was like a dam broke inside me and I wanted to keep pushing for more. Some of the things I've said and done recently, Ben would be so pissed at me. I just love you too much not to." He frowned and caught his lip between his teeth.

I felt like this was an information overload. There was so much to try and understand and I couldn't reconcile how terrible and alone he must have felt. He'd lost his baby, his fiancée and his freedom all in the same day and the one person he should have been able to count on, me, was missing in action. I was such a bitch and how he could still claim to love me after what I'd put him through, I had no idea. I needed time to think and get things straight before I spent the rest of my life trying to somehow make this up to him. "I need you to go Trick."

His face fell and I knew he had misinterpreted my intentions but I could feel the panic rising inside me and I needed to be alone. He nodded stoically and left with only a soft peck on my forehead. I didn't have the will or the energy to call after him and explain. I just sat still and stared out into the garden, my mind racing.

Chapter Eighteen

Two days passed without any sign of Trick. He must have spoken to Ben because there was no sign of the interrogation either. When Ben dropped a heavy thick brown envelope into my lap, I couldn't help but think it was from him, that he'd sent me something so he could still let me know he was there for me even if I'd asked him to keep his distance. I ripped open the top excitedly, stealing myself for the romantic gesture that lay inside. The contents slipped out on to the table and I frowned as the disappointment hit me.

"What did you get?" Ben craned his neck over to my pile.

I flipped through the contents and didn't know how to feel. "Err, it's from Leo. Moto GP VIP tickets, flights, hotel rooms, the lot." He'd stuck a green post-it to the front that just said ‘Leo x’. It really was a ridiculously sweet gesture; particularly as I’d pretty much just run away from him last time we spoke.

Ben whistled. “Wow. That is some gift. He must really like you. How many tickets are there?”

I held them up. “Two.” He raised an eyebrow expectantly. “Am I crazy for even thinking about going?”

Ben laughed. “No, not at all. You need a break from all this shit B.” He waved his hand at the world in general. “Obviously I should probably come with you. Y’know, just to make sure you’re alright.” He looked away sheepishly and I knew he was dying to grab the tickets right out of my hand.

I grinned knowingly at him. “Oh right, just to look out for me, that’s definitely what it is.”

Ben fell on his knees in front of me. “Beth, I swear to God, if you don’t give me one of those tickets I will never speak to you again.”

“Okay fine, let’s go.” He jumped up and kissed my cheek.

"You are the best sister ever." Ben rifled through the details excitedly, exclaiming in approval every time he turned another piece over.

Leo had actually thought of everything for what was essentially an invite to a weekend away in Germany with him. I liked the fact that he'd sent two tickets, knowing that I wouldn't go if it was just me and him. My phone was in bits on my bedside table so I asked Ben for his phone so I could put my SIM inside and get Leo's number out and call him.

"Hey Leo, its Beth."

"Wow. That was quick. I'll have to remember that in future when you don't answer the phone for two months all I have to do is send you free stuff and get you to call me instead." He chuckled, making me smile.

"Yeah, sorry about that, I've been kinda otherwise occupied." I really didn't want to have to explain myself.

"Hey don't worry about it. I'm just glad you finally did call though. Are you gonna come this weekend?"

I really appreciated the way he hadn't demanded answers, Andy would have done. "Actually, yes, so long as my brother can come too."

"I sent two tickets; they're yours to do with as you please. Although I have to admit to being pleased to hear you say 'brother' and not 'boyfriend'." He sniggered awkwardly and I didn't do anything to set the record straight.

"Well, I guess we'll see you Friday night then." I hung up before I could say anything else, like denying I was engaged to a man who meant everything to me. Ben shot me a questioning look with a thumbs up and when I nodded, he did a little geeky dance. Sometimes my brother was a total nerd.

"So do you want me tell Trick where we're going?" He looked down at the floor, embarrassed.

"He hasn't spoken to me for days; I doubt he'd even notice I was gone." There was a little resentment in my tone that I hadn't meant.

Ben came and sat down next to me. “He’ll notice B, trust me. You asked him to give you space and that’s what he’s doing. If you don’t want that then just tell him.”

I sighed. “I know how crazy this is gonna sound Ben but I don’t want to tell him. I want him to fight for us. I want him knocking on the door all day long demanding to see me. I want him to want me.” I looked down at my hands, fully aware of how ridiculous I sounded.

Ben tilted his head all the way back until I could see his Adam’s apple straining against his skin. His face was contorted in frustration when he looked back to me. “Beth, you’re asking him to be someone he’s not. Trick is not the man for grand gestures and throwing himself around like a lunatic. He’s a man of few words. He’s quiet and reserved and stands back from the crowd. He will love you for the rest of your life with a passion you will never see again but asking him to go against what you’ve asked him to do, that’s not him babe. If you push him away, then he will let you. Not because he doesn't love you but because he will always obey your wishes, no matter how much it tears him up inside. If you could have seen him after Annie…. He stayed away for you babe. He did fucking time for you. He gave up everything, for you. I think it's about time you decided what you want from him. I know you've been through a lot and we all want you to get well and find your place in the world, believe me. But you're breaking his fucking heart Beth. If you're having doubts about him then you need to man up and be honest with him. It's not fair any other way. He deserves better than that." Ben pushed off his chair as soon as he'd finished speaking and made to leave. He stopped in the doorway and half turned to face me. "Please Beth, do the right thing." He went upstairs and I was left alone with my depression.

It was a strange feeling. I knew that I was in love with Trick and even when I'd thought things were different, when I thought he wasn't mine, I'd still loved him. The truth was that I was terrified of hurting him, of not being enough for him and worst of all, that I might forget him again. I knew I'd been through two terribly traumatic events and they had culminated in me creating my own reality but what was to stop that happening again? Trick and I had nothing in common; most of what he said to me was like another language. Also, more than anything I knew that Trick wanted a family and I didn't even know if that was possible for me now. Maybe Ben would know. I dragged myself up the stairs and hovered around in his doorway until he looked up.

Sat across his bed with a book, he looked like another person. I didn't even know he had any books. His eyes were on me but the rest of him was still in place where he'd been when I came in. "What do you want Beth?"

I ran my tongue over my lips, trying to get some much needed moisture into them so I could speak. "Do you know if I can have kids? Y'know, after what happened?" I figured if anyone would know, it would be Ben.

His eyes fell down to the crisp white pages but I could see he wasn't reading. He tossed the book to one side and patted the bed for me to sit down. I knew how he felt about telling me things I hadn't remembered and was hoping that the dilemma that posed was the only thing postponing his answer. His eyes flicked over my face and I saw devastation behind them. I knew what his answer was before he even opened his mouth. "They had to do a hysterectomy to save your life."

I didn't react because I had been preparing myself for that response since I first walked into the room, I was sure then that I had known that all along. "Does Trick know?"

Ben nodded once. I couldn't believe that someone who wanted a family as much as Trick did would still want to be with me; surely it would be a deal breaker for him. "He loves you Beth. He'd do anything for you."

I curled up in a ball next to Ben's side and closed my eyes. He picked his book back up and started reading again which I was immensely grateful for. I didn't want to talk about it; I just wanted to be done with it. I made up my mind to go to Germany this weekend and talk to Trick when I got back.

I reached out and pushed up Ben's book so I could see the cover. It was 'The Count of Monte Cristo'. I smiled as I thought about the hundred times we'd read that book as children together. Ben and I huddled under the duvet with only a tiny torch for light as he acted out each part with reckless abandon. When we were little, it had been his go-to thing in times of crisis, always pulling it out and letting the words fortify him when he needed comfort. I found myself wishing that I had something like that, something tangible that I could always reach for to calm me down. As I snuggled against Ben's chest, I realised that he was my Count of Monte Cristo. He had never let me down and would always be there, no matter what.

Chapter Nineteen

Friday night arrived before I had time to blink and I still hadn't worked up the guts to speak to Trick about my trip. When Ben came home and raced up the stairs to pack, I followed him in the hope I could get him to do it for me. I was such a chicken.

"I spoke to Trick today." I exhaled in relief, glad that my brother was not only a mind reader but some kind of saint. "He's got a gig and will be gone for two weeks. I didn't tell him about this weekend as I thought you should do it." He glared at me clearly displaying his obvious disappointment that I hadn't done it yet.

"I will tell him Ben, I just don't know what to say." I threw myself face down onto his bed. "Do you think he'll be mad at me?"

Ben carried on throwing his clothes into a bag. "I guess that depends doesn't it?"

I lifted my head slightly to face him. "On what?"

He came and sat next to me. "Beth. You know I love you and I'm going on this damn trip because well, who would turn that shit down? But I'm worried. You barely know this guy and he seems to have gone to a lot of expense to see you again. Do you really think he's just gonna wave at you and then send you on your way at the end? He wants more from you B. The question is, what are you going to do about it?"

I grabbed a pillow from under my head and hit him with it. "Alright Mister Smarty-pants Know-it-all. Who knew you were such an expert on relationships all of a sudden?"

He laughed. "Not relationships B, just men. I know I'd be expecting something from a girl I'd just arranged an all-expenses paid VIP trip for. You can't honestly tell me you believe this guy just wants to be friends with you?"

I sighed heavily thinking about Leo's boyfriend question. "No, I know he wants more than that. Am I taking advantage of him if I just go on the trip and don't do anything with him?"

Ben looked pensive and thoughtful for a long time before he answered. "It's not like he sent you the tickets with a note that said 'if you come on the trip then you're my girlfriend' or anything. You need to take a break and enjoy yourself for a little bit. All I'm saying is, just be careful. Even if you do want something to happen with Leo, it's not fair to Trick to be less than honest with him. Call him B. Please?"

I wasn't happy about my stupid brother and his stupid insightful comments but I nodded anyway. I grabbed Ben's phone and slunk away into my room. I stared at my sim card for ages before pushing it into Ben's phone and pressing call. Trick answered right away.

"Hey beautiful. How are you?"

I couldn't help but smile at the sound of his voice. "Not too bad I guess. Ben says you've got a gig?"

"Yeaaahhh. I didn't want to take it but it was too much money to pass up babe. Are you mad at me?" he sounded genuinely worried I might be.

"No of course not. You have to work right? Ben and I are going away this weekend too."

"Really? I spoke to him earlier and he didn't say anything. Where are you going?"

I grimaced and then spoke really quickly hoping that it wouldn't sound as bad. "This guy sent us VIP tickets and flights for the Moto GP in Germany this weekend."

"Wow. That's amazing. I bet Ben is bouncing around like a kid in a sweet shop right now."

I giggled. "Yeah he's pretty excited." He hadn't seemed to pick up my mention of a 'guy' who I had painted as some sort of magical ticket deliverer rather than a really hot man who clearly wanted to be more than an overeager postman to me.

"It'll be good for you to get away for a bit. You need a break."

I hate myself. "Thanks. So who's the gig with?" Why am I changing the subject and avoiding telling him the truth?

He laughed. "It's kinda cheesy actually but it's for Abel Armitage. He needs a drummer for his UK tour."

I rolled my eyes. I didn't think Abel Armitage was cheesy at all, I thought he was a pop God. He had so many number one singles and I would happily sing and dance to all of them at any time of day or night. He definitely wasn't Trick's kind of music though. "Wow, that's really great. He's big deal." And totally droolworthy. And like Justin Bieber famous.

"Yeah, I guess so. You wanna see if I can get you tickets? You could come backstage and meet him if you want?"

I repressed a squeal. "Oh my God yes! That would be awesome."

"I'll see what I can do then. You can see me backstage too if you want?" Although I couldn't see his face, I knew that one eyebrow was cocked suggestively in my general direction.

"Oh really? Well I suppose that wouldn't be so bad."

Trick laughed and was just about to say something when Ben appeared in the doorway. "Time to go B." He tapped his watch impatiently like he had been ready for hours, which I knew wasn't true.

"I've gotta go. Call me, okay?" I put extra emphasis on the okay hoping that he would get the hint and actually realise that I wanted him to call.

"I will Tink. Have a good time, but not too good." He chuckled as he hung up.

I grabbed my bag and dashed downstairs where Ben was already pacing impatiently. He held out a new phone for me and I kissed him on the cheek in thanks. He really was a great brother. "Come on then, let's go." He instantly brightened now we were on our way.

Chapter Twenty

The hotel Leo had booked for us was beyond beautiful. Just walking in made me feel ashamed that I might be thrown out immediately for not being classy enough. My Converse squeaked against the marble floor with every step, while the people in front of us managed a gracefully superior clickety-clack. I grabbed for Ben's hand and hoped he wouldn't do anything to draw attention to us. The concierge greeted us brightly and handed over our keys but it wasn't until we were in the lift and I checked the card to see what floor to press that I realised we were in the penthouse. I pressed the rather imposing looking 'P' button and held my breath as we rocketed up to the top floor.

The doors opened onto a magnificent foyer complete with crystal chandelier and mandatory fruit bowl. There was a large sitting room that was almost the size of our entire downstairs with five separate bedrooms, all with on-suite bathrooms and Jacuzzis. It was beyond ridiculous. "Are you sure you haven't slept with him already B?" Ben popped his head out of one of the bedrooms, his face full of concern.

I bit my lip awkwardly. "It's too much right? I should tell him we're going to just find another place to stay?"

"Are you fucking joking? This is amazing! I just worry about what he's going to want as payment for it. You must be one hell of a first date!" He sniggered but didn't drop his frown.

"Fuck you Benjamin. Just because all you get from girls is herpes." I spat back at him teasingly.

"You bitch. You will totally pay for that later. Come on snarky, let's go eat." He pulled at my wrist but I wanted to get changed first, not wanting to walk through the hotel dressed like a tramp. Ben sensed my reluctance. "You're fucking hot. Deal with it. Come on."

He tugged again and I relented although when he went straight to the hotel's restaurant, I stopped dead and made myself as heavy as possible.

"Can't we just go somewhere else?"

He rolled his eyes. "You mean somewhere less posh?" I nodded and he looked around at the clientele. "Fuck 'em. They probably all have sex with their socks on. Now come on, I'm starving." He pulled again and refused to head in any other direction so I gave in to prevent a scene.

A few diners glanced our way and took in the sight of my brother. Even in scruffy jeans and a t-shirt he was still strikingly handsome and I caught one woman actually lick her lips as she eyed him like he was a steak. I shot her my most sarcastic smile and she hurriedly turned away. I raised my eyebrows when I saw the prices on the menu and glanced at Ben nervously. "Don't worry about it B. We'll charge it to the room." He cocked his grin at me and I knew he was feeling mischievous. I purposely ordered the most expensive thing on the menu in a moment of sheer daring. Ben always brought out my devilish side.

We'd just had our main brought over when I looked up to see Leo standing next to me, patiently waiting for me to notice him. I smiled at his kind face, his blonde hair flopping over one eye. "Hey Leo." He smiled but didn't say anything. "This is my brother Ben." I gestured to Ben who held out his hand.

"Pleased to meet you Ben. I'm…"

"I know who you are. You're Leo fucking McCarthy! Wow, you are an absolute legend." Ben was grinning so wide I was worried his face might split in two. He gestured eagerly for Leo to take a seat and then subjected Leo to at least twenty minutes of hero worship while he blubbed on about how great he was. It was kind of sweet really but I could barely eat anything with Leo sitting so close. He smelt like fucking Christmas.

Eventually Ben turned to find a waiter to order another drink and Leo took his opportunity to speak to me. "So, hi." He smiled the knowing smile that said ‘sorry about that, my attention was always intended to be entirely on you’ and my stomach fluttered slightly.

“Hi.” It was such a tiny word for everything I wanted to say to him.

“I’m glad you came.” His smile dimmed slightly for a moment as he looked at me and I knew there were a million things he wanted to say too.

“It was a very generous gift, thank you.” I suddenly felt really nervous and the thought of watching Demi Moore in Indecent Proposal came to mind causing me to have to stifle a giggle.

He frowned slightly trying to understand me. “Not really but I’m glad you like it. Can we talk later?”

His eyes narrowed with his question but Ben was on him again saying something about something he just remembered that was spectacular, diverting his attention from me. My new phone vibrated in my pocket and I pulled it out as they were talking. It was from Trick. I felt the urge to tilt the screen slightly so it was hidden from view and suddenly felt like I was having an affair but I wasn't sure who with.

Hey beautiful. Did U get there OK? I miss U. Xx

I flicked my eyes to Leo who was currently engaged in conversation with Ben about crashes. I bristled slightly, thinking about Leo's accident but he didn't seem concerned. He seemed to feel me watching him and glanced at me with a wink. I looked back at my phone quickly in embarrassment.

Just having dinner + then going 2 crash. Miss U too. Xx

I did miss him and we were having dinner so I hadn't lied exactly.

Sleep well Tink. I'll call U 2moz. Xx

I slipped my phone back in my pocket and felt it press against my leg as a guilty reminder of everything I was doing wrong. Every time Leo smiled at me and my breath caught in my throat or I thought about talking to him later and maybe running my hands through his soft blonde hair, I felt like such a bitch. What the hell was I doing?

I didn't doubt that Trick and I were in love and that he had been everything I needed him to be for a long time. Part of me just wanted one night where I didn't have to carry around all the baggage and history that came with being me and Trick. He'd held me after I'd tried to kill myself when I watched my mum bleed to death. He'd killed for me when that bitch had killed our baby. He was everything to me but sometimes I just wanted to be normal. Not the girl with the messed up past and the tangled memories. All Leo knew about me was that he liked me and why the hell couldn't that be enough, just for one night?

When the bill came, Leo signed his name without even looking at it and passed it back without so much as a word. His eyes settled on Ben. “Would it be okay if I talked with your sister alone for a while?”

Ben instantly tensed and looked at me. “If it’s alright with Beth then sure. But I’d rather you didn’t leave the hotel.” His tone was firm and commanding despite his obvious respect for Leo.

Leo nodded his consent and turned to me. “Is that okay Beth? We can sit in the bar and you’re free to leave whenever you want.” He smiled openly and I knew he felt like he needed to be on his best behaviour, not just for Ben but for me too.

I nodded and flashed a smile at Ben so he’d know I was okay. He left me with a hug and a kiss and whispered in my ear. “I’m not sleeping until you’re back, I can be here in less than a minute.” He tapped the phone in my pocket before turning back to Leo with a warning glare and telling him he’d see him tomorrow.

We took a seat in the bar area and Leo was deliberate in choosing the chair furthest away from me in the small alcove we sat down in. “I wanted to apologise for overstepping the mark on our date. I feel terrible about it." His brow furrowed and I could see it had affected him.

I shrugged. "It wasn't your fault, I was dealing with some shit and it just surprised me that's all."

He sniffed and tipped his chin in the direction of my hand. "You weren't wearing that before."

I looked down at my ring and bit my lip. "It's kind of a long story." I gave him an apologetic smile as he rubbed his hand across through his stubble.

He leaned forward suddenly more intent than before and rested his elbows on his knees. "Beth look, here's the thing. I like you, a lot. If you tell me there's nothing here then I'll just have a good weekend and I'll walk away. But I think there is something here. I don't know what's going on with you and this guy but if you were with me then I promise you, everyone would know what was going on between us. You wouldn't be flying off to other countries with some other guy. I would make sure you knew that the only way for you to exist was if you were less than ten feet from me at any time. And I would fight every fucker that ever even looked at you if I had to. I want you to be mine Beth, I want every single piece of you there is to give." He leant back in his chair and rolled his bottom lip between his thumb and forefinger as he studied my reaction.

I couldn't take my eyes off him. He was mesmerizingly sexy and firm and his eyes were demanding my immediate obedience and submission. Trick never looked at me this way, his eyes were always filled with longing and desire dampened by disappointment and chagrin. Private parts of my body clenched in response to Leo's eyes and I swallowed. "Leo…. I…." My mouth was dry and I couldn't get any words out, not that I would have a clue what to say if I could.

He waved his hand horizontally to stop me from trying. "Beth. Come to my room with me. Let me show you how good it can be." It wasn't a question or an invite, it was a command. My legs stood me up and took a step towards him before I knew what they were doing. His jaw remained firm and set as he stood up and placed his hand in the small of my back to lead me away from the bar and up to his room. We didn't speak in the lift or when he pushed his hotel room door open and gestured for me to step inside. I was instantly reminded of a poem by Mary Howitt that Ben used to read to me as the door clicked shut behind me.

'Up jumped the cunning Spider, and fiercely held her fast.

He dragged her up his winding stair, into his dismal den,

Within his little parlour -- but she ne'er came out again!'

Chapter Twenty One

Leo's eyes roamed my body as he sat on the edge of the bed and undid his top button. "Take off your clothes Beth." My fingers were trembling but I lifted my top over my head and let it float down to the floor. I tugged at the zip on my skirt and hugged my chest as I stood before him in my underwear. I felt like I had somehow surrendered all control of myself to him when I walked in the room and now his husky voice and deep chestnut eyes were the only things keeping me focused. I couldn't explain what was happening but I felt like I needed it somehow. I needed someone to tell me what to do and help me put aside all the fear and anxiety that was inside me.

He crooked his head in a gesture making me take a step towards him like my body was responding to him unconsciously. Achingly slowly his head dropped down towards mine and our lips brushed together softly. My mouth parted on a gasp and he took the opportunity to slide his tongue inside to stroke against mine. My whole body trembled, partly with desire and partly in pure fear as he moved back and looked at me.

His hands pushed firmly between my thighs, parting my legs and with one swift movement lowered my panties to the floor. The pads of his thumbs stroked my scars slowly as the corners of his mouth twitched upwards. As his thumb brushed against my entrance a shudder ran through me and I lurched forward awkwardly. Leo's hand pressed against my stomach and steadied me before he grabbed my waist and manoeuvred me on to the bed. He hovered above me and the desire in his eyes made me feel unbelievably sexy and lascivious.

Leo rocked back on his knees and looked at me with an intense desire burning in his eyes, his blonde hair framing his face. I was overcome with a sense of self-consciousness and hyper-awareness at what was happening. I am Jack's cold sweat. My heart was pounding heavily and I struggled to catch my breath. Sitting up suddenly, I clasped at my chest in a panic. Leo's face dropped instantly from passion to concern. "Shit Beth, are you okay?"

I shook my head and fanned my face with my hand as he rushed to get me a glass of water. I took a sip but my throat was closing in tightly and I choked. Leo's hand grazed against my back lightly in comfort and as my hand trembled; my engagement ring clinked against the water glass. I stared at it like it was trying to poison me. "I have to go." I grimaced realising that this was almost exactly how I had ran out on him last time. As I gathered my clothes up and pulled my top over my head, Leo made no move to stop me.

I practically fell through the door of the penthouse and Ben swooped down on me like Batman. His hands ran over me quickly in inspection and his shoulders lurched into a tense state as soon as he caught my panic stricken eyes. "Holy fucking Christ Beth. I knew I shouldn't have left you with him. Did he hurt you?" Ben glanced up at the door with vengeance raging across his face. I shook my head quickly and he relaxed slightly. "Come on baby; let's get you in to bed."

I lay down and stared at the wall. What the hell had come over me? I had been so desperate to push back all the crap in my life I had been inches from having sex with someone who wasn't Trick. I felt cheap and dirty and really queasy. My stomach rolled over and I threw myself across the room and into the bathroom, barely making it through the door before I saw my dinner hurtling across the floor. I fell to my knees in front of the toilet bowl and heaved until there was nothing left, laying my head against the cool porcelain and letting the tears fall. I felt so stupid and pathetic. I closed my eyes and must have fallen asleep there as the next thing I knew Ben was lifting me and sliding me in between the sheets.

He sat down beside me the next morning and stroked my face gently making me smile. “Do you wanna go today?” I chewed on my lip knowing that this was something Ben would really enjoy and not wanting to let him down.

“You should go, I’m just gonna hang out and sleep. I feel really tired.”

Ben’s face was full of worry. “Do I need to hurt this prick? I will y’know.”

I shook my head. “No, it’s not his fault that I’m a fucking mess is it? You go, have a good time.”

He planted a kiss on my forehead. “Okay but I’ll call you in a bit and check in so answer your phone. Try and get some sleep.” He pushed my phone into my hand so I wouldn’t have any excuse not to answer and left with a final concerned glance behind him.

As I stared at my phone and tried to work out what I would say to Trick, a memory tugged at the corner of my mind. I lay back and closed my eyes, letting it flood in and take me over.

My Own Worst Enemy

Trick's bed was undoubtedly my favourite piece of furniture in the world. Considering he was a boy, he always seemed to have clean and pressed sheets that billowed up into a cloud of freshness when I sank into them. His mattress was the perfect amount of soft and firm and I could happily spend my whole life lying on it with him next to me. I nestled further down into its soft embrace as he rummaged through his drawers. "Are you sure you haven't seen it?" He was almost frantic now.

I shook my head sleepily. "No babe, I promise. Just come to bed and we'll find it later." I patted the sheets next to me and he looked at me with genuine conflict.

"I want to do that so bad but I can't Tink. I can't be late again, they'll kill me." I giggled guiltily, aware that every day this week he had been late to practise because I had made him come back to bed. He ran his hands through his hair and mumbled to himself as he retraced his steps to find his missing wallet. I knew exactly where it was but I wasn't about to tell him that and lose my valuable Trick time.

"Just for five minutes baby, then I'll help you look I swear." I lifted the covers and flashed him a shot of my naked body. He groaned deeply and slid in beside me.

"You are the devil baby." His lips were on mine in a second and his hands were already snaking their way down my body as his hard cock pressed insistently against my thigh. I smiled into his mouth as I pulled him on top of me.

"Why do you love me?" I spoke just as he nudged the tip inside me and his body froze and his head jerked back sharply as he looked into my eyes.

He pushed himself deeper, opening me up to him as he stared at me. "You're beautiful, you're funny, you're perfect and best of all, you're all mine." He buried himself fully inside me and I tensed slightly against the strain. "I love you Tink, say you're mine."

I looked into his grey eyes and melted before him. "I'm all yours baby, always." He grinned as he thrust himself against me over and over, never once taking his eyes from mine.

My Own Worst Enemy

A tear rolled slowly down from my eye and pooled in my ear. I sniffed back the sob and sighed heavily knowing that Trick deserved someone who was better than me. Kinder than me. Less fucked up than me. In fact, anyone who wasn't me. He was just too good for me in every sense of the word. I would never be able to give him a family and I couldn't even stop myself from going to another man's hotel room and getting naked. I slipped the ring off my finger and placed it reverently on the pillow beside me. I didn't deserve his love and he didn't deserve to be treated with such disrespect.

I stumbled over to my bag and rummaged around until I found what I was looking for. I crumpled down on the floor, my back against the wall and pressed the tip of the scissors against my wrist. I deserved this. I deserved to suffer. I deserved the pain.

"Beth? FUCK! Beth?" Ben was shaking me, his face was red and his eyes were alert. I blinked and stared at him, confused at his behaviour.

"What? Leave me alone." I tried to push him away but my body felt heavy and my arm wouldn't lift on command.

Ben slapped me, hard. My cheek tingled sharply and I struggled to focus. "Beth, get the fuck back in the game. Look at yourself." He held my wrist up in front of my face and I squinted to look at it. The angry slashes I'd carved into my skin were gaping and blood was seeping from them freely. "Can you stand?" He picked me up and placed my feet on the ground as I tried hard to concentrate on what I was meant to be doing. I felt the carpet under my toes and tested the weight of my body on them as he held me. I nodded once and he led me at a snail's pace into the bathroom.

"Ssss..sorry." I knew it was pathetic but it was all I could manage. Ben wet a cloth and pressed it to my arm, the coolness of it ran through me and I shivered in response.

"If I can get this to stop bleeding then I'll take you for something to eat." His brow furrowed as he looked at my arm but he seemed to relax slightly, confirmation that the bleeding had stopped. Ben took off his t-shirt and ripped it up into strips and started tying them around my wrist carefully. “Jesus Beth, this shit is killing me here. I don’t know what to do to help you.”

I swallowed. I couldn’t let Ben give up on me. “I’ll be better. I promise. Don’t leave me.” I choked on my words and repressed another sob.

He touched my chin lightly with the pad of his thumb. “I’m not gonna leave you am I? That’s just ridiculous. I just wish I knew how to make you better.” I looked at him sadly. I wish I knew that too.

Chapter Twenty Two

Ben sat next to me on the plane, his jaw set firmly and his eyes stilted with anxiety. Every time I glanced at him, I saw the muscles tightening in his face and his heart beating a thunderous rhythm through the vein in his neck. The hostess flirted shamelessly with him but he was oblivious, even when her breasts were inches from his nose. His hands bunched tightly into fists in his lap as he stared at the back of the chair in front of him like he was going to lunge for it at any second. I hated that this was what I'd done to him but I had no words of comfort or consolation for him, I was too busy dreading speaking to Trick again. He had sent me three texts that I had deleted without reading, feeling too full of guilt to allow myself the pleasure of his thoughts.

My Own Worst Enemy

I rubbed my arm firmly, the healing skin now achingly itchy, a reminder of how weak and good for nothing I was. Ben's eyes followed my hands with a grimace. "I think you should go back to Risemoor." His tone was flat and resigned.

I opened my mouth to protest, to say anything to change his mind. I looked into his eyes and saw his broken heart and just nodded. This time it wasn't for me, it was for him. He needed to be able to live a normal happy life without the constant worry of what state I would be in when he got home. He deserved this and so I gave it to him.

He drove me there as soon as we landed, unable to articulate any words that would even for a moment express how he was feeling. He checked me in and hugged me softly before walking away without looking back. I wanted to run after him, to scream at him, to tell him how sorry I was, beg his forgiveness but it was too late. The numbness inside me was already seeping across me and when Steve appeared in the doorway with a solemn look, I just shrugged.

He flashed me a disdainful smile and held the door open for me to walk through. As it clanked heavily behind me, I could practically feel my body shutting down. I just wanted to crawl into bed and wait for it all to be over. Steve had other ideas though and dragged me into his office, gesturing for me to sit down. I plopped heavily onto the sofa and folded my arms, pulling my knees up to my chest with a scowl. His eyes wandered to my bandaged wrist.

"Want to tell me what's going on?" His tone was light and casual.

I shook my head. "Not really."

He nodded and leant back in his chair. "Alright then. Tell me what's going on." He smirked at his own grammatical trickery making me cluck my tongue in annoyance.

My Own Worst Enemy

"Ben needs a break from me." I rolled both my wrists out dramatically in a 'voila' motion indicating that my presence was not my own decision.

He tugged at his lip as he studied me. "Why do you think that is?"

I raised my eyebrows in incredulity. "Well who the fuck wouldn't?"

A smile tugged at his lips. "You think you deserve to be left behind don't you?"

I nodded. "Of course, I'm a bitch." Steve just stared at me, no questions, just waiting. I felt the barriers threatening to break, the bravado and the attitude crumbling under his stare. I dug my fingertips into my leg to force me to keep it in place. My throat locked under the pressure of holding back words that were threatening to come spilling out at any moment. My eyes felt like they bulging in their sockets. As I opened my mouth to take a breath the tiniest whimper escaped and the whole fucking mess came hurtling out.

“I fucked up so bad this time. I nearly slept with someone just to let them take the control away from me. I wanted someone else in charge of my actions so badly, I craved it. This will be the end for me and Trick, I know it. He’s too good for me; he deserves someone better than me. How can I ever look him in the face again knowing what I did? This time when I cut, it wasn’t like before. I didn’t want the pain to take the other feelings away; I wanted the pain because it was mine. I should be hurting, I should be fucking destroyed. How dare I do what I did? What sort of fucking monster am I?” I looked hopelessly into Steve’s passive face as the tears streamed down my cheeks in tiny salty rivers.

He let me cry for a long time before taking a deep breath and smiling sadly as my tears dried into the occasional hiccupped sob. “Beth, you’re being too hard on yourself. The trauma you’ve experienced is more than enough for one person to have to deal with. The fact that you can even acknowledge it at all is major breakthrough for you. Everyone in your life loves you and cares about you. Let them in and let them help you rather than trying to take it all upon yourself. Why are you trying to do this alone?"

I squeezed my shoulders tightly. "I don't want to be a burden." As soon as I'd said it I felt something inside me break. My mind blocked out everything around me and I was consumed by a memory so fierce that I could barely breathe, too terrified of it.

I was hiding in the kitchen cupboard. It was dark, too dark and the smell of bleach and damp filled my senses making my stomach churn. My breath caught in my throat as I heard him shuffling into the kitchen, knocking something over that sprinkled glass everywhere with a tinkling sound that echoed around the empty room.

"Princess? Where are you princess?" His words were slurred from the drink but pleading and pregnant with a million unsaid threats. I whimpered and clasped my hand over my mouth sharply. It was too late, he had heard me. His feet shuffled again and came to a halt in

front of the cupboard. I wished Ben or my mum were here. They'd gone out to get Ben's new school shoes and left me with him. I'd silently begged them to take me with them but he'd been so insistent that we'd have a good day together, lifting me up onto his knee with a grin.

He yanked the cupboard door open and was dragging me out by my wrist. I felt a sharp pain run up my arm as I struggled against him but he was so big and strong. He pulled me up and sat me on the kitchen table, his breath heavy with whiskey as he stared at me with glassy eyes. "That wasn't very nice now was it princess? Hiding from your dad like that?" He sneered at me as he wobbled slightly. I wanted to scramble back across the table and put some distance between us but I knew it was no use. He licked his lips and a globule of drool dripped from his lip and onto his shirt.

Moving closer to me, his hand grabbed for my leg and moved it aside so he was standing between my thighs. I swallowed back the bile that was rising in my throat and closed my eyes. If I could take myself somewhere else, make myself think about something else then maybe I could get through it. I tried to focus on the time that Ben and I went to the park and we played with a kite he'd found. I brought to mind the colours of it and the way its tail fluttered in the wind. But his stink was unbearably strong. Every time I thought I was pushing it away, it lingered longer, his body pushed against mine and I felt suffocated. He groaned and pulled out of me, his hand curling tightly around my throat.

"Go to your room you fucking little whore before I have to explain to your mother how you made me do this. How you came to your poor defenceless dad and wouldn't stop tormenting me with your tight little pussy. Don't make me break her heart." He pushed against my throat and flung me to the floor. I scrambled across the tiles and made it upstairs before he could come after me again.

I opened my eyes and saw I was curled into a ball. My stomach bubbled and I forced myself to sit up. The movement made me retch and bile rushed out of my mouth. Steve's eyes were concerned but not shocked by any means. I instantly despised the fact that everyone knew more about my life than I did. "I want to go home."

Steve nodded. "Good. I was hoping you would say that."

Chapter Twenty Three

To my surprise Steve led me straight out to reception where Ben was already sat waiting for me. My brow crinkled in confusion as Ben's arm curled around my shoulders and he planted a kiss on the side of my head. "I told you I wouldn't leave you B. You just needed someone to talk to." I let him walk me to the car and buckle me in, waiting for him to take his seat and start the engine before I stared at him.

"I thought you'd given up on me."

He frowned and concentrated on the road ahead. "I'd never give up on you, when you will understand that? You're my sister, I love you, stupid." He chuckled at my ridiculousness.

I knew he'd told me this before, many times, but I just couldn't believe it. How did he keep putting up with me? A painful thought tore at my heart and I spoke without really thinking about the consequences. “Did you know about dad?”

He flashed a look into his mirrors and swerved across the road, turning in at the side and clicking his hazards on before pulling the handbrake sharply. Unclicking his seatbelt, he turned to look at me, his eyes full of despair. “Don’t call him that. He doesn’t deserve that. Do you know what he did?”

I shook my head, knowing I had barely grazed the surface. My hands curled tightly in my lap and my voice trembled. “I know he did things to me.” My chest tightened, the smell of whiskey assaulting me.

“I wish you could keep that stuff out B, more than anything else.” He ran his hand through his hair. “He’s gone now; you don’t have to worry about him, okay?”

I caught Ben’s tortured soul reflected in his eyes and a million images flashed before me. My dad putting his hands on me. Ben and Trick walking in and my dad’s shocked face. Ben dragging him across the room. My screams as they beat him, kicked him, blood everywhere. My dad's face sneering at me lecherously from the hallway as he plunged the knife into my mother's chest. Ben's hands covered in blood as he sat on the bathroom floor sobbing. It came back in such a rush of feeling that my whole body was shaking. The two men in my life would and have killed to protect me, at all costs, even giving up their own sanity for me. I reached out for Ben and he quickly unbuckled me and pulled me into his lap. We sat there for a long time, not speaking, my body quivering with tears that refused to fall. I couldn't cry for that man, I could only let the hurt and pain wash over me and through me until it was gone. "I need to see Trick; will you take me to him?" I needed to get this over with quickly before I changed my mind.

Ben secured me safely before pulling away. When I saw we were headed towards home I shook my head. "Please Ben? I need to see Trick."

He put his hand lightly on my knee. "I know B. I called him as soon as we landed and told him you hurt yourself. He drove straight back. He's waiting for you." The guilt I felt was only compounded by the fact that Trick had now given up a job for me and probably trashed his reputation too.

"Did you tell him about Leo?" I felt panicked that he would already be angry with me. I needed him to listen to me first.

Ben shook his head and I allowed myself to breathe. "It's not my place. Tell him when you're ready." He shrugged it off like it was nothing but I knew Ben felt my guilt on his own shoulders too.

"I will." I sighed and stared out of the window contemplating the impending worst conversation of my entire fucking life. "Have you got cigarettes in here?" I looked around me as if they would magically materialise. Ben leant forward and opened the glove box. I reached in and took the packet and the lighter and held one to my lips. He pushed the centre console button for the electric windows and the sudden rush of air made the flame on the lighter flicker slightly as I cupped my hand around it.

I inhaled deeply and let the nicotine glide through my lungs. My hands were shaking and I had to fight back the tears, concentrating solely on the act of smoking to steady me.

When Ben finally pulled up in our driveway I snatched up the cigarette packet knowing I would need it. Ben watched me but didn't comment, staying seated as I went to get out of the car. I frowned at him. "You not coming?"

He shook his head. "No. You guys should talk. I'm just gonna get some stuff done. My phone's on though." He grimaced, obviously wanting to say more but knowing that it was futile. I smiled at him in an attempt at calming him but I don't think it worked. I sucked air into my lungs before stepping towards the house reluctantly.

Trick was sat at the kitchen table when I entered; his smile wide and open even though he made no move to come towards me. I walked over and sat in the chair opposite him, unable to make eye contact with him. He reached for my hand but I recoiled knowing his touch would only make this harder.

“Tink? Talk to me baby.”

I reached into my pocket and retrieved the engagement ring, sliding it over the table towards him. His face fell instantly into a look of pure horror. “You need to take this back.”

He shook his head firmly and pushed the ring back across to me. “No fucking way. It’s yours.”

“I don’t deserve it Trick.” I don’t deserve you. I slid it back to him.

He nudged it back to me with the tip of his finger. “Tink, you deserve more than I can ever give you. What’s going on? Talk to me.”

I swiped at the ring and it flew sideways across the table, balancing precariously on the edge. “I can’t give you what you want. You should be with someone who can.”

He sat back in his chair and folded his arms. “And what exactly is it that you think I want?” His tone was firmer now, bordering on angry.

My lip trembled. “I can’t have children.” The tears threatened to come but I forced them back with a sniff.

He grimaced painfully. “I know that babe. I don’t give a shit. All I want is you.”

I shook my head. It wasn’t enough. “Trick, even the one thing I thought I had given you, it wasn’t real. It was a lie.”

He frowned. “What the fuck are you talking about?”

I choked, this was too hard. “I thought I’d given you my virginity but even that was… tainted.” I squeezed my eyes closed.

He shifted in his seat. “Tink, fuck that. I’ve told you before; if it’s not given willingly then it’s not gone. I was your first and you know it. You feel it. I know you do.” He reached for my hand again and held it firmly so I couldn’t pull it away.

The contact between us was trying to break me. My resolve was faltering and I longed to creep across the table and into his arms. I allowed myself a glance into his beautiful grey eyes. There was nothing but pure love there. I had to hurt him. If I didn't then he would never leave me. I knew that was the truth. There was nothing about me that would make him turn away, except one thing. I needed him to leave me. If he didn't then he would ruin his life for me. All his hopes and dreams and happiness would slowly be eroded by the poison that was me. I would burn a hole through him until there was nothing left.

I focused on his eyes and concentrated hard on making my voice cold and dispassionate. "I slept with someone else."

His hands released me like they'd been electrocuted. He pushed back in his chair and stood in a violent movement and glared at me. "Like fuck you did. When?" His hand fisted down onto the table heavily, causing the ring to jolt upwards and tumble to the floor with a merry little jingle.

“Friday.” My tongue darted out and wet my now dry lips.

He stared at me, willing me to take it back or say it wasn’t true. It wasn’t true but it was close enough. If I hadn’t have freaked out then it would have been and that was all I needed to know. I kept my gaze steady, refusing to let my swirling emotions take over. He swallowed; his voice was shaky and broken as he pointed his finger at me accusingly. “You have five seconds to take this back Beth. Tell me now that it’s not true.”

My shoulders were shaking from holding back and every nerve ending was tingling and on edge. “It’s true Trick.”

His face visibly crumpled in front of me, hanging loose between his shoulder blades. When he came back up to look at me, there was nothing but coldness there. He held his hands up in submission. “Fuck this shit; you’re fucking crazy do you know that?” I nodded, completely agreeing with him. “I’m out Beth. I can’t do this shit anymore.” He shook his head and walked away. As he got to the front door, he paused and turned to look at me. “I fucking loved you. I would have given you the fucking world Beth.” He sneered at me, hatred and loathing boiling from him before opening the door and walking through it.

Watching him go, my resolve finally broke and I scrambled after him, skidding on the kitchen tiles. As I flung the door open I saw him on the driveway with my brother. Ben was pushing him backwards and they had a look of bulls locking horns about them.

Trick was shouting. “Let me go Ben. Your fucking sister is batshit crazy.”

Ben pushed him again, trying to steer him back towards the house. “She’s hurting. She doesn’t understand what she’s doing. Don’t do anything rash.”

Trick shook his head and made a move to step forward but Ben held him in place. “She understands having another man’s dick inside her though. No Ben, just no. It's too much. I can put up with her shit but not that."

I wanted to run to him, stop him from hurting. Tell him it wasn't true but I couldn't. This was better. If he hated me then he'd move on. Ben glanced over at me and then back to Trick, his voice lower now. "It's not what you think it is. Please Trick, just think about it."

Trick paused for the briefest of moments before turning to look at me. His face was filled with love for less than a millisecond before it turned to revulsion. He faced Ben with a shake of his head. "Can't do it man. It's over the line and you know it." With those words, he pushed past Ben and walked off down the street.

Ben's eyes followed him hopelessly as my legs crumbled beneath me. I let the emotion take me now; filling the empty void that Trick's departure had left in my soul. This was better for him, he needed this. I just had no idea how I was ever going to recover.

Chapter Twenty Four - Trick

I wooed the shit out of that girl. Not at first of course. But I knew from the first moment I laid eyes on her that she was it for me. I left their house that night and flopped down on the sofa in front of my dad with the biggest grin on my face.

"What's got you all smiley? You're acting like a woman." My dad never did feelings. Or any type of emotion really. I'd never even seen him angry.

"I just met the girl I'm gonna marry."

His big bassy laugh echoed around the front room but it was hollow and empty. "Well at least you accomplished something today. Now take that ridiculous grin of yours elsewhere. I'm trying to watch my shows." He waved me off with a huge hand.

My Own Worst Enemy

In bed that night I lay awake thinking about her. I knew there was no way I could ask her out yet. We were too young for dating and her dad would never go for it. He was a miserable bastard and I won't lie, I was terrified of him. One day soon I knew I'd be as tall as my dad and then the odds would be in my favour.

We hung out as friends and I got to know her. Under the guise of spending time with Ben, I slowly pulled her closer to me until we were in a place where we could reasonably be seen together alone. Her smile made my heart beat that little bit faster and her brown eyes were like deep pools that sucked me deeper every time I looked into them.

On her sixteenth birthday, I made my move. They didn't have a party and there weren't any cards on the windowsill or even a cake. In fact, it was just like any other day. But I knew the truth and I was determined that my girl was going to have a special day. I waited by the school gate for them to walk up and just like every morning when I saw her, she took my breath away. Her long brown hair flowed around her face like a waterfall, being pulled in a hundred directions by the November wind. She pulled her scarf tighter as a particularly vicious gust swept by her. Ben caught my eye and nodded once, his part in my master plan already locked down. Moving a few steps ahead of her he shot me a wink.

I grabbed her around the waist and pulled her behind the wall as she let out a scream of surprise before my hand went to her mouth. "Shhh. It's me. I'm kidnapping you."

I released her mouth as her eyes sparkled up at me with excitement. "Trick? Where are we going?"

"No questions. Just come with me." I tugged on her hand and she followed me with complete confidence.

It took twenty minutes to get to the Thames on foot so I entertained her with stories that I could remember from television. If I didn't know exactly how they finished then I made them up but she didn't seem to mind.

My Own Worst Enemy

When we finally arrived, I helped her climb up onto the wall of an abandoned building so we could hang our feet over the edge. I loved coming here because when you looked down it seemed like you were standing right on the river. "Look down."

She did as I asked and her smile spread even wider as her tiny shoes dangled over the edge. "It's like I'm walking right on the water."

I grabbed for her hand and pulled it in to my lap. "Tink I need to ask you something."

She shuffled along the wall so our thighs were touching. "Okay, ask away."

My thumb stroked her palm gently. "Do you like me?"

She thumped my shoulder with a fist. "What? Of course I do dumbass." Her giggly little laugh was like angels singing.

"No I mean do you like me, like me?" I squeezed her hand and met her eyes. They changed rapidly from amusement to understanding and then to something else, like a fire had been lit inside them.

Her lip trembled and her voice was suddenly a breathy whisper. "Do you like me, like me?"

I held her gaze for a long time, trying to convey the depth of my feelings to her with just a look. Words were not my strong point and I had no idea how about poetry or any of that bullshit. So I settled for action. Moving towards her, I captured her mouth with my own and kissed her like my life depended on it. I knew she'd never kissed anyone and neither had I so I had no idea if any of this was how it was supposed to go down. What was certain was that my body thought it felt right and responded by moving almost on top of her, my cock even trying to make its case heard. Her hands wrapped around my back as I lay her down and settled between her legs, our kiss deepening and becoming needier by the second. It was as if two years of foreplay had led us to that moment and now we were absolutely desperate to take things further.

We didn't of course. No girl of mine was gonna lose her virginity on a brick wall in full view of everyone. But when we did, it was perfect. Even if I did have to wait a heck of a long time for it to happen. But being with her was enough, just breathing the same air as her was enough.

The problem with taking our relationship to the next level was that when she was lying naked in front of me there were things she couldn’t hide from me. Like the pale scars on the insides of her thighs that she'd try so hard to cover up with blankets. Ever since her mum died it had been happening more regularly and it scared the shit out of me. There'd been too many times when I’d taken her to the hospital to get fixed up and one time when she nearly died. A part of me wished that I'd told Ben earlier, got her some help quicker but I don't think any of it would have helped in the end. None of it would have stopped Annie from doing what she did.

Chapter Twenty Five

Annie was always a bit weird. She wasn't really friends with anyone, preferring to hang around on the edges of every group. One thing she was deadly certain of were her feelings for me. We had physics together and would always end up as lab partners. At the time I thought it was just weird co-incidence but in hindsight it was more than likely just another one of Annie's manipulations. She'd do anything to be near me, once creeping into the showers after PE and trying to blow me.

Tink hated her and had every reason to. Annie was far from subtle about her advances, particularly in front of Tink. She acted as if Tink didn't exist. When we left school, things only got worse. Annie would show up at my house naked, crying and banging on the door at all hours. She'd make up stories about us sleeping together and spread them around until they got back to Tink. Once she even broke into my house and was lying in my bed when I got home. The only thing I ever worried about was how Tink would feel about it all. For the most part, she took it well but I could see how much it hurt her. Especially when our friends would bring it up in conversation with secret looks that said they thought I might have actually done something. Considering the extent of her obsession, most people would presume something had to have happened. But they were dead wrong.

There was only one time when it nearly drove a wedge between us that was almost too big to fix. When we were twenty two I'd had a huge piece done on my back. It was epic. My back had remained pretty clear until then, mainly because I couldn't see it and I liked to appreciate the art of the ink on my skin. When I'd seen Ben working on the scene in his sketchpad, I knew I had to have it. It was a stage, a band and the crowd. But it was amazing. Like words could never do it justice. It came alive from the page, transporting you right there in to the moment as if you could hear the crowd roaring in your ears. It took Ben three months to finish it but it was totally worth it. The thing was a piece of art and deserved to be scraped clean from my skin and hung in a gallery.

Except Tink didn't see it the same way I did. Whenever I came home with a little more done, she seemed pissed off instead of elated or impressed. She would scowl at it and make 'hmmm' noises. When it was complete and I dashed back to show her, she started crying. It was beautiful and even I wanted to have a little sob every time I saw it but they didn't seem like happy tears to me. I pulled her on to my lap and stroked her softly. "What's the matter baby? Talk to me."

"Do you love me?" She had to stutter it out in between sobs.

"Of course I love you, you're my whole world." She was the only woman I'd ever really known and I had zero experience with this. Diffusing a crying woman was about as far down the lists of my talents as you could get.

"But you want to leave me, take off on the road and be famous." It wasn't a question and suddenly I started to understand things a bit clearer. Apparently laughter wasn't the answer because that made her cry even harder.

"Baby no. I like what I do. I like coming home to you as often as possible. There's nowhere else I'd rather be than right here. I'm all yours baby. I promise."

She sniffed back some snot. I loved her with all my heart but she was an ugly-ass crier. "But you love performing. That's why you got that on your back. To remind you of how good things can be."

I shook my head. "No baby. I got it because it called to me, because it's fucking beautiful. But nothing in this world is more beautiful to me than you are. There will never be anything that's as good for me as being right here with you."

I think she believed me. We had a few days of some pretty explosive sex where she seemed to be begging me with her body to never leave her. So the next week I was back on Ben's table getting more ink. I swore him to secrecy on this one, it was private between me and Tink.

I winced when I sat down to dinner and Tink was on to me in a heartbeat. I dropped my pants right there in the dining room so she could inspect me. On my left bum cheek I'd had the word 'yours' inked in. She laughed, I laughed. Everything in the garden was rosy. Or so I thought.

Two days later she was storming through my front door and frantically shoving her stuff into bags like her life depended on it.

"What the fuck is going on? Did someone die?" I was genuinely confused and had no idea what was going on.

She scowled at me. "Yes. Our fucking relationship you bastard." More clothes went into her bag as I tried to understand what could have possibly happened between this morning and now.

I grabbed for her wrist but she tugged free and I wasn't going to hurt her by holding on so I let her go. "Talk to me. What happened?"

Tears were pouring out of her and when she went back to packing I saw the fresh cuts on her wrists. This time I did grab her and held on far too tightly. "What the fuck is this?" I shook her wrist in her face and she stared back at me with blank eyes.

"How could you Trick? How could you sleep with her?"

My face crumbled into a frown. "Sleep with who? I've never slept with anyone but you. You know that. Why are you cutting yourself?"

She pulled back her wrist until I had no choice but to let her go and then threw her bag at my chest with all her might. It dropped to the floor with a dull thud. "Annie! You slept with Annie." As if too exhausted to worry about her stuff anymore she ran for the door.

"Beth wait!" I'd not used her name in years but it was enough of a shock to get her to stop, even if it was only briefly. "I swear to you, I didn't do it. You know what she's like. She's a lying bitch." Apparently that wasn't the right thing to say either because she shook her head sadly and left. I stood there in our room like an idiot. I didn't chase after her and I didn't call her. There was no heartfelt apology, there was just… nothingness.

It took me three hours to get it together enough to go and see her. As soon as I stepped through the front door and heard her soft moan, panic engulfed me. She was in the kitchen, slumped against the counter, blood pouring out of her. At the hospital she took one look at me and my blood soaked t-shirt and just shook her head sadly. "Just go Trick. I'll make my own way home."

I reached out for her hand but she jerked away. "I'm too angry with you. Please. Just leave."

I called Ben on the way out and made sure he went to get her. The whole house felt empty without her and I had no idea how to even start fixing the mess between us.

When I woke up the next morning, she was wrapped around me like a blanket, her face still stained red. Our eyes met and she just shook her head slowly. "I don't want to talk about it." And that was it, we never did.

Annie however, didn't stop. She pursued me relentlessly, without any boundaries. I changed my number a hundred times but somehow she always got the number and blew up my phone with messages. She loved late night visits to my house, sometimes just sitting outside, sometimes pushing love notes through the letterbox. I just presumed she was mental but I should have been paying attention. I should have done something about it. And for that, I will never forgive myself.

Chapter Twenty Six

I never thought that I would be attending my own child's funeral. I certainly didn't think that I would be escorted to it in the back of a police car, my wrists in handcuffs. I rested my head against the window and tried to shake off the feeling that my heart was beyond broken, shattered and irreparable. It wasn't just the fact that I had imagined a life for myself with Beth and the baby and then it was taken away, it was that I couldn't even share my grief with her. We couldn't comfort each other and learn how to live through it because she couldn't remember a single piece of it. When her eyes caught mine it was as if I was a stranger to her, a casual acquaintance rather than her whole world, her reason for being.

Ben had visited me two days ago and told me what she'd managed to twist in her mind. That Annie and I were in love and this was her funeral we were attending. It had almost broken me then, my body trembled under the weight of it and I had to be carried away like an invalid. It took every part of me to restrain my anger, to stop me from destroying everything in my cell, knowing that they would stop my day release if I stepped out of line. The pressure inside me built and built but I held it back, not wanting to jeopardize my chance to speak to her. I just needed ten minutes to tell her how I felt, try and impress on her that I'd be there for her so if things got better for her while I was away then at least she'd know how much I loved her still. I was absolutely terrified that I would be in prison when she got well and she would think that I'd abandoned her. My solicitor said I could get six years. I didn't know if she'd wait that long for me but I had to do everything I could and this was the only thing I had any control over.

We pulled up outside and PC Riley opened my door and surveyed me carefully, weighing me up. I knew what he was thinking. I was a big guy, six five was tall by anyone's standards and I was pure muscle. If I got out of hand, he wouldn't be able to hold me and he knew it. He sighed heavily. "Look, I know what this day means to you and there's been nothing but good reports on you. I'll uncuff you and stand back but don't mess with me or I'll make things very difficult for you. Do you understand me?"

I understood perfectly. A bad day now would ruin my chances of a light sentence and I couldn't afford to risk it. He was being really lenient with me and seeing Beth when I wasn't shackled would make things easier on her. There would be too many questions I couldn't answer. I nodded. "You won't have any trouble. Can I talk to my girl though?" He nodded his assent and uncuffed me, allowing me the chance to rub my wrists before stepping aside so I could get out.

Ben approached me slowly, aware that any sudden movements would not go down well. "Hey man. She's asking for you." He turned to Riley. "Is he okay to sit with her?"

Riley switched his focus between the two of us and I was sure he thought his day was getting worse by the second. All I needed was for him to catch sight of the twins and I was certain he'd be dragging me back into the car before he had chance to take another breath. "Sure. Just stay where I can see you okay?"

I exhaled slowly, the relief washing over me as I let Ben lead me through the church and over to Beth. Riley followed on behind but took a seat further down. I sat down next to her and she turned to me, her face a picture of agony and sadness.

"I'm so sorry Trick." She wrapped her tiny arms around my neck and I struggled to hold it together. She was feeling my perceived pain for Annie instead of her own. Her compassion for me was overwhelming and coupled with her proximity, I thought I was dying. Her scent was wrapped around me like a blanket and as my arms slid across her body, I shivered with need. There were so many things I wanted to say but I just couldn't bear it.

She held my hand tightly throughout the service and leant against my arm. I was frozen in place by her, unable to move in case she edged away from me. Now she was next to me, I couldn't bear to have her anywhere else. My body felt as if it was aching for her, incomplete without her.

Her counsellor had suggested the funeral as a way of helping her grieve, perhaps even come to terms with what had happened but it wasn't working. I could see it on her face that she didn't understand what was going on at all. I wished for her oblivion to rub off on me so I could close my eyes for one second and not have to see her lying on the floor covered in blood. Even the thought of it made me want to vomit and my chest heaved heavily, holding back the bile that was threatening to rush through me. She turned and smiled sympathetically, patting my leg in consolation. I wanted to pull her over to me, sit her on my lap and kiss her, help me to push back the pain and anger and desperation but I knew it would make her freak out. Ben told me how he'd tried to talk to her but she'd refused to believe it, breaking down and withdrawing until he had to act as if nothing had happened. I couldn't watch her go through that no matter how selfish I was feeling right now.

She got up at the end and mumbled to me about going for a cigarette. I felt her absence immediately but needed some time to collect myself before going to her. Once I was sure I could control myself I stepped over to Riley. "I want to go outside and talk to my girl. Is that okay with you?"

He nodded, noting the tension in my body. "I'll wait by the door for you. We need to be getting back in the next twenty minutes though." I sighed and walked slowly outside.

Beth was sat against a wall, her body slightly turned and hidden from passers-by. It wasn't until I got closer that I could see what she was doing and my stomach turned over. There must have been a hundred tiny little cuts on her thigh, blood trickling softly out of each one. Her face was completely impassive like she wasn't even aware she was doing it. "Tink?" I kept my voice soft and low, not wanting to startle her.

Her face was heart-breaking, full of pain, so clearly thinking that the horrified look on my face was nothing to do with her at all. "Hey Trick. How are you feeling?"

I lit a cigarette to force my hands to do anything other than pick her up and run away with her, forcing her to listen to me until she knew the truth. "I've been better." I let out a tiny giggle at how ridiculous this whole situation was.

"Is there anything I can do for you?" She looked up at me so sweetly.

Oh God yes, a million things starting with not cutting yourself anymore and finishing with you remembering everything and then running in to my arms so I can hold you and love you for the rest of our lives. "No, Ben's got me covered." She stood up and put her arms around my neck and I clung to her tightly, not wanting to let go. I had to speak now or the words would never come. I held her back slightly, just enough so she could see my face. “One day I’m going to wake up and not feel so sad. Things will be better and I’ll not be carrying all this shit around with me and I’ll be able to be the man you need me to be. When that day comes I promise you, I’ll ask Ben’s permission and then I’m coming back for you. You and I will be together forever.”

She blinked a few times but it was as if I had never spoken. I closed my eyes resolutely and started to turn away. The pain in my chest was almost unbearable and if I didn’t put some distance between us then I didn’t know what would happen to me. I caught Ben’s shoulder as I walked away. “She’s been cutting herself. Look after her please?” His face was a mirror of mine, full of pain and desolation.

Riley opened the car door for me and I slid inside, compliantly holding my wrists up for him. He clicked the cuffs and closed the door. “She really doesn’t know what happened does she?” He sounded sorry for me, but I couldn’t bring myself to talk about it. I didn’t want to risk getting angry, not when I was so close to sentencing, so I allowed myself a single shake of the head. “I’m sorry.” He didn’t say anything else on the drive back and I was thankful for that at least.

When the cell door finally closed behind me I collapsed on my bed and silently sobbed. There was nothing worse in here than showing weakness of any kind but I just couldn’t contain it any longer. If I didn’t cry then the anger would take control of me instead and that wasn’t an option.

My sentencing was swift and they took into consideration my time already served and impeccable behaviour. They gave me four years but with an option to be out in eighteen months if I proved I was a good inmate. The first three months were the hardest. I was an intimidating looking guy and there was a definite need for people to prove themselves around me. They faced off and taunted me, trying to get a rise out of me but I stayed silent and kept to myself. Once a guy did actually hit me. I let him and walked away, only going back later when I was sure no-one was looking and delivering my revenge. He spent four weeks in the infirmary and suddenly the interest in me died down and I was left alone.

Chapter Twenty Seven

Ben came to see me every week without fail. After a few months, I started to become braver in our conversations and ask about Beth. Part of me didn't want to know but I would only torture myself every night thinking of what could possibly be going on. He sat across from me with a concerned grin, wanting to be supportive and helpful but feeling torn up inside.

"Has she started to remember yet?" I felt anxious even asking and could barely stand to listen to his answer.

He grimaced. "No, not really." Concern crossed his face and he looked at me steadily. "I want to tell you something but I don't want to make things harder for you. Do you want to hear it?"

I nodded sharply and tensed, holding my emotions tightly inside me. If he told me she was seeing someone then I was prepared for it.

"I don't think she understands why but she asked me to do a new tattoo for her. It's an ace of spades on her hip. I just thought you should know." He shrugged and looked down uncomfortably.

I'd been holding my breath but I hadn't realized, suddenly gasping for air. My eye caught my own tattoo on my forearm and I held it out. "Did you make it the same?"

He nodded. "It's an exact copy, I made sure. Look man, I don't think it means anything exactly. She's still oblivious to everything but she couldn't explain why she wanted it, just that she did. Maybe it's just a coincidence."

My head moved slowly in agreement but I wasn't convinced. The very fact that this had happened meant something. In some small dark place in her mind, I was there with her; she just couldn't see it yet. "Do you think she'd come and visit?"

Ben flinched at my words. "And what would we tell her about why you're here?" He shook his head. "No man, it's a bad idea however you look at it. Don't rush her; she'll get there, one day."

One day felt like a really long time away. "Is she seeing anyone?" I inwardly cursed myself for asking; clearly I was a glutton for punishment.

Ben's face scrunched tightly and I could see him debating what to tell me. I didn't want to sit in here completely helpless while thinking about her out there with someone else's hands all over her but I had to know before it drove me crazy. "She is. The guy's a dick; Jay already had words with him." He smirked and I mirrored it, knowing that Jay's talks would have gone along the same lines as the one I wanted to have with this guy. "From what Jay said, I don't think it's gone anywhere, just a few dinners and some hand holding."

Well that wasn't as bad as I thought. I allowed a tiny piece of tension to ease. "What about the cutting? At the funeral it was like she didn't even know she was doing it." I leaned forward intently to keep my voice low. The last thing I needed was anyone picking up on it and using it against me later.

Ben's grim smile said it all. "I took her to Risemoor that day but it was a waste of time. She didn't know the place, like she'd never been there before. She couldn't even recognize that anything had happened. It was pretty scary to be honest. She's still doing it, I've found her passed out and bleeding a couple of times but she has no recollection of it. I just don't know what to do about it, I can't help her."

I swallowed back my tears, unable to show any weakness right now. "She'll start to remember eventually, just try and keep her safe until she does. There's no way she could keep me out forever."

"I really hope you're right man."

That day was the hardest for me. Back in my cell I struggled against my emotions, fighting to tame my pain and anger until I could lock it away inside me. I couldn't let them get the best of me because I could risk extending my stay and the longer I was away from her; the harder it was on all of us. I let myself become numb to it all, using her name as an endless chant so that I could focus on anything except the reality of my current situation.

When my review meeting finally came around and they stamped my form and told me I could go in a week, my heart stopped beating. I had served my time and paid my dues for what I did and now I was so close to being back with her. I'd spent eighteen months with little to do except work out and was more muscular now than ever, my hair closely shaved. I didn't think she would even recognize me now anyway, I looked so different. I kept my head down even further in the last week, not willing to jeopardize my freedom for anything. I have to admit to purposely committing certain faces to memory just in case I ever saw them on the outside, I knew it was petty but there was so much rage inside me now and I had to find an outlet for it.

Ben picked me up when I was released and took me home. I was relieved that I had someone I could trust who had paid my mortgage from my savings and kept an eye on everything for me. All the amenities were switched back on after he'd had them turned off when I went inside and he'd even been food shopping and filled the fridge. I couldn't tell if it was genuine brotherly love or a guilty conscience but either way, I loved him for it.

The first thing I did was crack open the top on a cold beer and take a sip, letting the bubbly amber nectar slide down my throat. Obviously Beth was top of my miss list but this was coming a close second right at that moment. I necked the rest of the bottle and opened another. "Can you fit me in later?"

His eyebrows raised in surprise. "You should never have a tattoo when you're feeling emotional. You know that. They're for life man."

I chuckled. “Have you seen me? I know they’re for life, wanker. Can you or not?” I rubbed my arm, already heavily decorated in tattoos like the majority of my skin.

Ben shrugged but still didn’t look convinced. “Well if I say no you’ll get some other joker to do it and I can’t live with myself if you get hepatitis or something so yes, I’ll fit you in.”

I pulled him in for a manly hug and slipped my arm across his neck. “Thanks man. Not for the tat, but y’know, for everything.” It wasn’t enough and it would never be enough but it was something.

“Don’t mention it. Come on; let’s get you inked up before I change my mind.”

He did an amazing job as always and I couldn’t help but stare at it before he wrapped it. All along one arm in beautiful Cyrillic letters, winding lazily around my other tattoos was a single word, ‘Tinkerbell’. I immediately felt better knowing it was there, like having her permanently etched into my skin was somehow a way of keeping her close to me. “Can I go see her?”

Ben winced as if I'd hit him. "It's not a good time man. She seems happy right now. Maybe in a few months."

I nodded but I couldn't say I agreed with his strategy. Keeping her from anything that might trigger a memory just seemed wrong. I knew he wanted to protect her but he was keeping her too close. "As soon as she starts to remember, I'm honouring my promise y'know."

"Just don't hold your breath, okay? She hasn't remembered anything yet and I don't know that she ever will. She seems to be okay with it and I don't want her getting worked up right now."

Ben was a good guy; I had to keep telling myself that. He'd done a lot for me, more than I ever should have asked of him. He loved Beth more than anything, I knew that. I'd seen it the day we walked in on her dad trying to rape her. His vengeance that day had been swift and brutal. I'd seen it the day we went to find his dad after he'd killed their mum. The red cloud descended across him and something completely snapped inside him. There was no limit to what he would do to protect her and I felt the same way, so I worried that the two of us, locked together in disagreement over her would be more than anyone should have to bear. If she ever got her memory back and knew that we'd spent this whole time fighting, she wouldn't be able to cope with it. I sucked it up silently and let him have his way, for now.

I did go and see her a few times, following her until I could 'accidentally' bump in to her and ask her to go for a coffee with me. She treated me the same way she did Jay or the twins, like an extension of her family. She was familiar with me, comfortable, but the love that had burned so brightly behind her eyes was gone. She was attracted to me, that much was evident, always touching my arm or staring at me when she thought I wasn't looking, but she didn't love me, not like I did her.

After three months of torturing myself, following her around like a creepy stalker and checking out her wet blanket of a boyfriend, I needed a distraction. I went out drinking and found myself a girl to take home. The next morning, I told her to leave. That night, I went and found another girl to take home and the next morning I told her to leave. It got to the point where I couldn't sleep alone but I couldn't bear waking up next to them either. A few really stupid ones came back on multiple occasions but I still told them to leave the next morning. I kept hoping that the sickness would start to subside but it didn't. I got a call about a six month tour in Australia and I took it just to get away and try and forget the pain that was my existence. When I came back, things were the same. I did a tour of the Midwest for three months, I came back and things were the same. Four months in Europe, things were the same.

Finally something happened. I came back from tour with some idiotic woman who had spent the whole time telling me how no-one really understood her. I understood her just fine, she was shallow and self-centred and ignorant and I told her so on multiple occasions while thrusting myself inside her. I felt ridiculous doing it, hated myself a little too but it was easy and stress free and it filled the time. I got back home, showered and changed and went straight out to meet the boys, feeling hopped up from the tour and in need of some fun.

Once she slipped into my arms, I could feel the change in her. Her body responded to mine in a way it hadn't done for years. As I pulled her on to my lap, her breath caught and I could feel her heart hammering a beat. Even if she couldn't remember me, her body could and that was enough for me. When I asked if she wanted to go home and she nodded, I knew I had to speak to Ben. This was my shot with her and if something happened before I spoke to him then things would go very badly.

We stepped into a corner of the bar and he could practically see it on my face already. "I'm asking. Tonight, I'm going for it." I held my arms out wide in a gesture of good faith but he wasn't ready to listen. He punched me right in the face without a word. My cheek stung and knew he'd split the skin. I had some unreleased rage but I wasn't about to start a fight with Ben if I could help it. Every muscle in my arms was straining to attack but I stayed firm and held back, keeping my arms out wide. "Ben, don't do this. I know you're only doing what you think is best for her but she remembers me."

Confusion and uncertainly crossed his face and he flicked a glance at Beth. "She doesn't. There's no way she does."

I nodded slowly. "You did not feel what I just felt. It's there man, she loves me." I kept my tone slow and steady, not wanting to show my frustration.

He chewed the inside of his cheek nervously, fists still ready to fly out. "I don't want her to get hurt." His eyes dropped to the floor.

"Do you really think that's what I want? I don't want her in any kind of pain but this is fucking madness. There's no way she can keep going through life not knowing what happened to her. I want to protect her as much as you do but we need to support her through it not help her keep it locked away. Please Ben, don't do this."

As soon as the words were out of my mouth, Ben's hand was around my throat and I was slammed back against the wall. I clenched my stomach muscles to hold me back from lunging at him. "Stay away from her. You'll make things worse."

I couldn't help but laugh and it only served to annoy him even more, his fingers curling tightly and obstructing my airway. Every word I spoke was a struggle but I made each one count. "You think this is the life she wants? Dating twats like Andy? You don't know what he's like; I've seen him with at least ten girls. She's lonely and she needs me. This is going to happen. One way or another, I'll make it happen, so step aside and make room before you lose her."

The pressure relented slightly and his face was softening slowly. "If I get even a hint that you're hurting her, I swear to God Trick, I will kill you." I nodded and he released me, holding out his fist for me to bump.

I put an arm around his neck loosely and leant in so I could be in no doubt that he heard me. “I’ll look after her, you have my word.” He didn’t answer me but his features were cloudy and disturbed. I knew this was eating away at him but I had no choice. Beth came before all else.

When I got her home, I wanted to ask her out. She stood between my legs like she had a million times and her tiny hands ran through my hair. My dick was so hard I thought it was going to explode in my pants. She was beautiful and vulnerable and perfect. Things between me and Ben were strained and if I went for it right now they would only get worse. I needed a few days to get my shit together and try and prove to her that I was good for her. If she didn’t remember me exactly then I was going to have to win her heart all over again and that just wouldn’t work if Ben and I were at each other’s throats. It was so frustrating, the one thing I wanted more than anything in the world was right in front of me and all I had to do was take it. I left before I could do any long term damage.

Shelley was on my doorstep when I got home in nothing but a long trench coat. I could see how tacky it was but right at that moment I needed something to fill the void so I took her upstairs and fucked her. Beth was the only thing in my mind when I did it but it didn't stop me from feeling any less guilty about it. I stupidly kept her around for a few days, only leaving the house once to go and satisfyingly kick the living shit out of that prick Andy. Shelley was one of those girls that never gave me hassle or asked me what I was thinking. She just waited around until I was ready for her again. I would have felt guilty about treating her so badly but there was no room inside me to care about another girl.

It calmed me to have her around, even if it was meaningless and going nowhere. Until Beth showed up on my doorstep in the middle of the night and Shelley was still in my bed. All I could manage was a phone call to Ben to come and get her. If Shelley hadn't have been there then things would have been different. I would have carried her up to my room and made love to her right there; she looked so ready for it. But Shelley was there and I vowed right then that there wouldn't ever be another girl in my bed again unless it was Beth.

Ben was pissed as hell when he saw the state she'd got herself in but I was silently overjoyed. She felt something for me, I could see the jealousy and the raw emotion across her face and I knew beyond all doubt that I could make her remember me if I just persisted. I told him I wasn't going to back down, that I loved her and that he better get used to it quick. He wasn't happy about it but there was no way I was giving up now when I was this close.

My intention the next day was to go and see her at work and push my luck a little, maybe even ask her out this time. I know I shouldn't have grabbed that guy but his dirty fucking hands were all over her and I just snapped. Compounded by the fact that snake Andy had told her about the beating I'd given him; I looked like a thug to her. She genuinely looked like she hated me right then. I said the wrong things, was too much of myself with her. The old Beth would have lapped it up and we would have celebrated my unashamed manliness with a hell of a lot of really wild fucking. This wasn't the old Beth. This was the new prudish, easily affronted and completely untrusting Beth. This was a Beth that didn't go through life with the knowledge that as an absolute certainty, I would always have her back. We were a team, always had been and when we were apart from each other, we just didn't work.

I stayed away from her after that, trying to give her the space she wanted. I needed her to calm down before I spoke to her again so she'd be receptive to me. If she was still angry then she'd just shut me down and I wouldn't get anywhere. As hard as it was, I was so glad I did. The next time I saw her, she practically dragged me to her bed. She only wanted the contact but I could feel it emanating from her body in waves – it was my contact she wanted. She nestled against me and fell asleep so quickly, her face shifting into a state of pure relaxation. Six of the most amazing hours of my life followed, lying there watching her sleep, terrified to move. I knew I had to leave before she woke up because I wouldn't be able to stop myself from kissing her if she looked up at me with those huge beautiful brown eyes.

Ben was waiting for me like the judge, jury and executioner, his arms folded firmly across his chest. "Please tell me you are not sneaking out of her room."

I fought back the impulse to be cocky and went with the truth. "She's sleeping. She just had me hold her, that's all." I grimaced as I spoke, feeling throughout my whole body the craving for so much more than that.

Ben sighed. "She loves you, doesn't she?"

I nodded. "Yeah she does, she just can't bring herself to accept it yet. Please don't ask me to stop seeing her again. You know how important our friendship is to me but she's my everything."

He scratched his head. "I won't, but I'm going to ask her how she feels and I'm going to tell her my concerns. She needs to choose this for herself. Don't push her in to it."

"I would never force her to do anything she didn't want to do. Not after…." The image of seeing her father spread out across her body while she begged him to stop was burned in to my mind for the rest of my life. No amount of alcohol had ever been able to wipe it clean.

Ben tapped the table while he thought about it. "Fine. Just go slow and don't fuck it up."

I left with slightly less heaviness in my chest knowing that Ben was starting to give in a little and that just maybe Beth was beginning to remember me. When Ben dragged her round to see me a week later, I knew for sure she remembered me. Not everything, she was still nervous and unsure but there was no doubting it now.

It took every single ounce of self-control to push her away from my lips that night. Every nerve ending was tingling and begging me to take her to bed. She wasn't ready though, I could see how difficult it was for her to start to remember even the tiniest piece of information, something that wasn't even fully accurate and I didn't want to risk breaking her. She'd just told me she was in love with me and that was enough. Still, it was full of foreboding. I should have kept her next to me all night but I didn't want to scare her away.

When she called me and asked if I'd slept with someone, my first instinct was to laugh out loud but then I wanted to break things. Things called Andy. I knew somehow it had come from him and as soon as I had proof I was going to crack his skull like an egg. When she hung up on me I didn't bother trying to call back and explain, she would never have listened. I sent a text to Ben and told him to go home. I had a feeling what he would find when he got there and I selfishly didn't want to see it. He would find her covered in blood and then would take her to Risemoor, I had no doubt in my mind once she hung up on me. It was a pretty prickish thing to do but I just couldn't look at her like that yet. It was too hard, too soon, too much like the day our baby died.

The first time I went to see her she confirmed my suspicions that Andy was behind the unfounded allegations she'd thrown at me. I went straight over to his as soon as I left her and slammed my fist right into his face.

"This is all your fault y'know. If it wasn't for you, Beth and I would still be together now." He held his bleeding nose as he spoke but it didn't make me feel pity for him.

"How the fuck do you figure that one?" I stepped further into the house and jammed an elbow into his ribs just for good measure.

"You realize she talks about you even when she's sleeping? Calling out your name at all hours? How the fuck was I ever going to compete with that shit? We could have been great together but instead she spent six months looking at my cock with utter revulsion. You did that to her and I fucking hate you for it." He spat at me, sending a heavy globule thick with blood at my cheek. It was enough for the red mist to descend as I flew at him. I knew I had to wrench myself free of him eventually and I did manage it in the end, leaving him broken and bleeding on the floor.

Chapter Twenty Eight

Being with this new Beth was like being chained to a rollercoaster and being forced to ride it over and over. She loved me, she put my ring back on her finger, then she hated me and wanted me to leave, then she loved me again. We were in a downward slide after she made me tell her about Annie and then pushed me away like an intruder. The old Beth would have let me in straight away, even if she was mad at me, she would have shouted at me for a while and then we would have made up. This version was like a fucking stone wall. She just shut down and that was it, end of conversation. I thought I was going to fucking die explaining all that shit to her and she just pushed me away and broke my heart in two. All I wanted was for us to be able to comfort each other, even if it was only for a minute.

My Own Worst Enemy

I couldn't see a way back for us so when I got a call about a job, I took it. The whole crew spotted what a miserable bastard I was being; constantly staring at my phone like it would give me the answers. They mostly left me alone and for that I was thankful. When she did call, I knew something was wrong right away. I could hear her deception in every word. I kept it light and casual, not wanting to scare her off but as soon as the phone was down, my fists were aching to hit something, or someone. I'd picked out the intonation about the guy she was spending time with right from the off and I'd be damned if I was just going to sit back and let her fuck her way around town until she came back to me.

I lit Ben's phone up a hundred times before he finally answered. "Jesus Christ man, I can't answer the phone when I'm driving."

"Well you should have pulled over then. What the fuck is going on?"

He drew in a breath and I knew what he was going to say before he even said it. “Trick, just give her some time okay? She’ll come back to you man.”

It felt like someone had reached into my chest and was squeezing my heart. “If she fucks that guy….” My hands fisted instinctively and fury raged through me.

“She won’t. I promise you, she won’t. She loves you.” He was remarkably calm in comparison to the way I felt.

“I can’t have another man’s hands on her Ben. Not again. It will fuck me up and then I swear the next thing I fuck up will be his fucking face.” My breathing was ragged and agonisingly painful now. Each breath like a dagger to my heart.

“Relax. Nothing will happen. She’s with me. I’ll look out for her. I promise.”

I hung up on him and went outside for a smoke. I needed to calm down and regain some control before I exploded. Every second that ticked by was a second closer to him and further away from me. It wasn’t just jealousy. It was more than that, possessiveness. She was mine. She'd always been mine even when she couldn't remember me; she'd still never given herself up to any of those guys. But now it was worse. She did have some of her memories, maybe not all of them, but enough. Enough to know what we were, what we meant to each other. If she slept with someone now then it would actually be cheating. It would be turning her back on everything we'd built together and I couldn't handle that.

I spent the night pacing the shit out of the floor, unable to sleep, wishing that I was there so I could wring that fucker's neck. When the tiredness took me over around five a.m. I started to think a little clearer. Guys wanted her, all the time. Fuck even Jay wanted her although he knew full well I'd break his legs if he touched her. I trusted her, always had. We were soul mates, destined to be entwined forever. There was no way she'd throw that aside and fuck someone else. I lay on my bed and closed my eyes, falling into a restless sleep.

When I woke up, I knew I was in trouble with this gig. I was easily a few hours late for rehearsal but it just felt so meaningless. I stared at my phone and pulled her number up. My thumb hovered over the call button but I couldn't bring myself to push it. If she wanted me then she was gonna have to tell me herself. When it finally rang, it scared the shit out of me and I almost dropped it.

"Trick? Things are fucked up man."

I sat up instantly at the sound of panic rising in Ben's voice. "What the fuck happened?"

"We're on our way back now and taking a detour to Risemoor. Shit man, I fucked up this time. I never should have left her."

"Left her? What the fuck are you talking about? Did she hurt herself?" I was already pulling my jeans on and looking for my keys.

"Yes, bad this time, the worst I've seen."

"I'm on my way back; I'll meet you at the house." I hung up and threw my shit in a bag. I'd already flaked this morning and was probably fired anyway so I just left without a word, climbing into my car and driving like a mad man. I had to be doing something and this was all I could think of.

I sat down at the kitchen table and waited, my knee bouncing nervously until I heard the key in the lock. She looked terrible, her hair was all stuck to her face and tears had burned lines down her face. I recognised it instantly and knew she'd remembered stuff about her dad. I smiled as warmly as possible and took her hand in mine. She pulled away and I let her, trying to give her space. "Tink? Talk to me baby."

She reached into her pocket and retrieved the engagement ring and slid it over the table to me. This was not going well. "You need to take this back."

I pushed it back to her with a shake of my head. As soon as she let go of that thing, she was letting go of us and I wasn't going to allow that. "No fucking way. It's yours."

"I don't deserve it Trick." Her fingers instantly pushed it back again and I could almost see the pain radiating from her.

I nudged it back to her with the tip of my finger. I needed to come up with something fast to stop her from doing this. "Tink, you deserve more than I can ever give you. What's going on? Talk to me."

She swiped at the ring and it flew sideways across the table, balancing precariously on the edge. "I can't give you what you want. You should be with someone who can."

I crossed my arms and sat back. She was so full of shit, how could she possibly think like this? I had done everything for this girl. "And what exactly is it that you think I want?"

Her lip trembled. "I can't have children." I could see the tears filling her eyes now.

I grimaced painfully. "I know that babe. I don't give a shit. All I want is you." It was the truth. I'd adopt a hundred kids if it would make her happy, just as long as I got to be with her.

She shook my head. “Trick, even the one thing I thought I had given you, it wasn’t real. It was a lie.”

I had no idea what she was talking about, it was like being stuck in a Dr Seuss book. “What the fuck are you talking about?”

“I thought I’d given you my virginity but even that was… tainted.” Her eyes closed and my heart broke for her.

I wished I could take it all away from her but I couldn’t. “Tink, fuck that. I’ve told you before; if it’s not given willingly then it’s not gone. I was your first and you know it. You feel it. I know you do.” I grabbed at her hand now, needing the contact between us more than ever. She had to know that none of that mattered to me; it wasn’t her fault that her dad was a fucking prick.

She stared at me for a lifetime and I silently begged her to yield, just let me take the pain away for a minute and hold her. Then her words hit me like a fist in the gut. “I slept with someone else.”

My darkest fear had just come true. She had to be lying, had to be. “Like fuck you did. When?” I slammed my fist down on the table imagining his face as I did it.

“Friday.” I fucking knew it.

She must be lying but I didn’t know why. I gave her one last chance to tell me the truth. “You have five seconds to take this back Beth. Tell me now that it’s not true.”

She looked empty and broken, reflecting everything I was feeling. “It’s true Trick.”

That was it. I couldn’t do this anymore. No way was I going through this fucking drama with her anymore. This wasn’t the girl I fell in love with. This wasn’t the woman who was holding on to my heart. This was some crazy fucking psycho bitch who had crept in and stolen the real Beth. “Fuck this shit; you’re fucking crazy do you know that?” She nodded. “I’m out Beth. I can’t do this shit anymore.” I shook my head and walked away. As I got to the front door, I paused and turned to look at her, wanting to say so much but to the woman I loved, not this mental case. “I fucking loved you. I would have given you the fucking world Beth.” I pulled open the door and stepped right in to Ben.

He pushed me back a step but I bulldozed my way through. “Wait Trick, please? Don’t just walk away like this.”

I carried on walking and he tried to hold me back. He put his hand on my chest and I had to hold back the need to punch him in the face. “Let me go Ben. Your fucking sister is batshit crazy.”

He pushed me again, trying to steer me back towards the house. “She’s hurting. She doesn’t understand what she’s doing. Don’t do anything rash.”

The time for rash was long gone. “She understands having another man’s dick inside her though. No Ben, just no. It’s too much. I can put up with her shit but not that.” It was true, my Beth would never do this to me. I could handle this new version and all her fucking lunatic behaviour but not this way.

Ben lowered his voice and looked into my eyes. “It’s not what you think it is. Please Trick, just think about it.”

I wanted to believe him and for a split second, I think I did. I turned and saw her standing in the doorway and my stomach turned. She wasn’t the woman I loved anymore and I knew every second with her from now was going to be a fucking nightmare for me. I shook my head. “Can’t do it man. It’s over the line and you know it.” I made it to the end of the road before my legs gave out on me. I had walked out on her for good and there was no going back.

Chapter Twenty Nine

This wasn't like last time. When I'd come out of prison, I'd stayed away from her because it was what she needed to get better. Now I was staying away from her because the crazy bitch had ripped my heart out and stomped all over it. For two months I lived on my sofa with a bottle of whiskey as my new girlfriend. Ben and the boys came round nearly every day to make sure I was still alive. It was Jay who let slip she was dating that prick she'd fucked. I wanted to kill him. No, I wanted to kill him and make her watch. No, I wanted to kill her. No, I wanted to kill everyone and watch them die in agonising pain. I fucking hated everyone.

Slowly I started to leave the house, take jobs, shitty ones though as my reputation was fucking trashed and turning up drunk every time wasn't helping improve it.

Four months passed me by, then five. A few times I considered burning off the skin on my arm so I wouldn't have to constantly look at the reminder of everything I'd lost.

Then I saw her. I hadn't been looking for her, in fact I'd been doing a pretty good job of avoiding everywhere I'd ever expect to find her. She was with that pixie friend of hers that drove Ben mad, I couldn't remember her name but it was something like 'plop' or something as ridiculous. They were across the road from me, talking excitedly and I couldn't help myself, I had to be closer to her. I was about to cross the road when I realised they were stepping into a bridal shop. My phone was in my hand and pressing call before I could even fully register it.

"Hey man. You okay?"

"Is there something you want to tell me Ben?" I kept my eyes trained on the shop, refusing to look away.

"Shit. How do you know?" At least he had the decency to sound cut up about it.

My Own Worst Enemy

"Well let's see. Perhaps because I can fucking see her trying on wedding dresses right at this very minute. When were you going to tell me?"

"Honestly? I wasn't. Nothing good could come from it." Ben was my best friend but sometimes he could be a real prick. He always thought he was doing what was best for Beth but in reality he was making things more difficult. His need to protect her was overriding any thoughts of common sense.

"Fuck you." I hung up and stormed across the road. My phone began buzzing in my hand but I ignored it. I paced up and down outside the shop for a few minutes, my hands running desperately through my hair.

I caught sight of her as she stepped out of the changing room and it took my breath away. She looked stunning. Beyond beautiful. She smiled sweetly and the old Beth was stretched across her face. My Beth.

I was fucked if I was going to let this fucking prick take my girl away from me. She was mine. All I needed was a plan. I had nothing.

Chapter Thirty - Beth

I looked down at my dress. There was no denying it was beautiful. The intricate lace across the top was handmade and Ben had joked to anyone that had asked that it was blind nuns working late into the night that made it possible. I stifled a smirk at his humour. He pushed the door open gently and smiled at me. He was breath-taking in his suit. “You look beautiful babe. You ready?”

I cast a glance around the room to see if I’d forgotten anything and my heart pulled inside my chest heavily. “I am making a mistake Ben?”

He stepped further into the room and took my hand. “Beth, this isn’t what I imagined for you either but you love him right?” He bent his knees to force me into eye contact.

I shrugged. “Yeah, of course. But….” I frowned, unable to articulate my feelings clearly.

“He’s not Trick.” It was statement that I couldn’t help but agree with. I nodded and slid my top lip under my teeth. “Leo’s a good guy. A bit weird but hey, who isn’t?” He waved a hand dismissively and I giggled. “You can still change your mind you know. Hell we can go and find Trick right now if you want?” He smirked mischievously and I knew he would if I agreed.

I shook my head firmly. “No, this is for the best. Trick’s moved on and so should I.”

Ben shook his head and frowned. “You’re wrong y’know. He hasn’t moved anywhere B. He’d take you back in a second if you just told him you were sorry.”

I searched his eyes for some sign that he was lying but there was only honesty there. “I messed up Ben. The things I put him through are just too awful. He won’t want me now and if he did, why wouldn’t he say something to me?”

Ben sighed. “Because he’s a stupid stubborn mule. I’ve told you enough times, he won’t chase you; he needs you to go to him. Do you want to?”

I closed my eyes and thought about the last few months. My memories had come back slowly but I was sure there were still things I couldn't recall. Sometimes out of nowhere a new memory of us together would float over me and my heart would break all over again. Every single day with Trick had been right out of a fairy-tale. He'd loved me with every piece of himself and I'd hurt him so badly. He deserved to be with someone who could be the woman he deserved. He deserved more than my broken shell.

After the shock and devastation of having my heart torn in two, I spent more and more time with Leo, learning to trust him. He was so different to Trick but it was what I needed. He was demanding, controlling, firm, but in a good way. He didn’t let me get inside my own head. He stopped me from analysing and destroying everything. He loved me and cared for me but it was different. It took a few months for me to let him in but when I did he just took the pain from me and sealed it off inside his own heart for me. All the hurt and pain, all the horror and fear. He said he kept it for safekeeping, locked away deep inside. It felt safe with him, secure.

Leo had never given up on me, not like Trick did. He'd fought for me even when I'd pushed him away and refused to go. I shook my head and stared at Ben. "I'm ready, take me to Leo."

Ben's eyebrows raised but he didn't say anything else. He held out his arm for me and escorted me down the corridor. The wedding march started to play behind the doors and as they swung open, I caught my first sight of Leo beaming with pride as he took me in. I squeezed Ben's arm tighter and he bent his head to whisper to me. "Don't worry babe, I've got you." My heart beat thunderously in my chest with each step but I kept my eyes focused on Leo and my future.

When Ben handed me over to him, my hands were shaking but Leo held me firmly. "You are the most beautiful thing I've ever seen." I let his words wash over me and fortify my resolve. This was what I needed, what was best for everyone.

The vicar started speaking but I wouldn't take my eyes from Leo. I feared that any break in contact would have me running towards the nearest exit and I just couldn't afford to do that. Leo suddenly blinked oddly and sweat pooled between our palms. I opened my eyes wider to be able to tune in to the vicar's words. "….just impediment why these two people should not be married?" There was silence and then nervous laughter rang out through the church. When nothing happened, Leo exhaled deeply and smiled again. I'd not realised he was waiting for someone to speak.

"Very well. So, do you Leo…." His speech was interrupted by the church doors banging open heavily. Our guests took a collective intake of breath and all heads turned to the doors. I suddenly wished that mine hadn't.

Trick was storming up the aisle in a suit. Well, he had the remains of a tuxedo on but the bowtie was hanging around his neck and his shirt had three buttons undone. There was no jacket. His hair was much longer than I'd ever seen it and hung messily around his stubble streaked face. He looked like he'd been sleeping in a bin and as he got within a few feet of us, I realised he smelt like he'd been sleeping in a bin behind an off-licence.

Leo stepped protectively in front of me but Ben was one step ahead of him, placing his palm firmly against Trick's chest. "Don't do this man, she's made her choice."

Trick looked over at me angrily. "Like fuck she has. She needs to hear me out first."

I glanced nervously at our guests who were resolutely silent and looking on as if this was some fascinating soap opera. I took a step towards Trick and lowered my voice. "Trick, you're making a scene. Please just go home and sleep it off."

I could see frustration in his features but he shook his head. “No, not until you listen to what I have to say.”

The vicar cleared his throat behind me but I ignored him. I grabbed Trick by the arm and pulled him to the side of the church, feeling every single pair of eyes follow us. “Fine, you have two minutes.”

His eyes scanned across my dress hungrily. “You look beautiful.”

I sighed. “One minute thirty seconds.”

He held his hands up with a smirk. “Fine. Don’t marry this prick.” He jerked his thumb back in Leo’s direction who was now being restrained by Ben who seemed to be speaking softly to him, hopefully reassuring him that I would come back in any moment. “Marry me. Or don’t marry me, just don’t marry him. I love you.” He shook his head. “No, that’s not right. I am you. Without you, there is no me. I know I’m a stubborn dickhead but I fucking love you. Just give me a chance to prove to you that I can be who you need me to be. I fucked up Tink. I never should have let you go.” He swayed slightly and a fire lit behind his eyes. Bending forward, his lips touched mine. I struggled to keep my mouth shut tight as his kiss became more insistent and needy. His hands slipped around my neck and pulled me into him.

I mustered all my strength and pushed against his chest, sending him stumbling backwards. His hand flew out and held on to a chair for support, his face full of shock. “Fuck you Trick.” I spat the words at him and stormed away towards Leo who was now a picture of agony under my brother’s tight grasp.

Trick’s hand shot out and pulled me back. “No. You can’t go. Tink please?” He fell to his knees, tears falling from his eyes. My heart broke with a desperate need to comfort him. He felt the change in me and pulled me down into his arms. I softened slightly and sank against him, the familiar feeling of him pressed against me lulling me into a dreamlike state.

There had been so many nights when my body had ached to be pressed against his. I had picked my phone up to call him so many times but I knew that he was better off without me. Now seeing him like this, I wanted to make it easier for him, I didn't want him to suffer any longer. As I knelt there, I realised that I was suffering too. Leo had been there when Trick hadn't but it had all been a façade. Like my missing memories, I'd allowed Leo to fill the emptiness inside me. I allowed myself to pretend that my life with Leo was a reality. In truth, there would only ever be one man inside my heart. One man who could ever mean anything to me. And here he was, in front of me, begging me to love him.

I pulled back slightly and looked at him. "Why do you call me Tink?" I had no idea why I needed an answer so badly but I felt like the course of my whole life was perched on a knife edge dependant solely on the answer he would give me.

He blinked in confusion and then smiled. "You're my Tinkerbell. My magical little pixie who sprinkles me with fairy dust and helps me think happy thoughts." He shrugged like it was the most obvious thing in the world. My lips crashed against his suddenly and I realised I was the one who had moved. My fingers were in his hair and my tongue was in his mouth, a need greater than any I'd ever felt overwhelming me, needing to melt into him before he disappeared in a puff of smoke.

There was an atrocious wail snaking its way to my ears and I recognised it clearly as the sound of Leo's heart breaking. I managed to get to my feet and was immensely relieved that Trick's frame helped to support me. I made my way over to Leo, my feet feeling heavy and full of lead. Every head in the church followed my movements silently. Leo was swaying and broken in Ben's arms, not even able to hold himself up. He could barely look at me but then he seemed to shake it off and glared at Trick with renewed determination.

"Don't fuck it up this time man." He snorted and then turned on his heel and walked dejectedly down the aisle. We all watched him go, everyone too shocked to speak or move.

As he stepped over the doorway, Trick slid his arm around my waist. "Come on then, let's go."

I frowned at him. “Go where?”

He grinned mischievously. “Well by my reckoning, we’ve got a wedding reception to get to.” He swept me up in his arms as if he were about to carry me over the threshold. “Come on then you nosy fuckers, let’s get wasted.” He glared out at the guests causing Jay and the twins to stand up and whoop excitedly. Leo’s mum looked like she’d just sucked on a lemon but for the most part, everyone followed behind us like Trick was the Pied Piper.

Trick bent his head to kiss me again as he carried me back down the aisle and I kissed him back furiously. There was no doubt in my mind now that this man was my whole world and there would not be a single day in my life from now on where I would let him forget it.

Epilogue - Two Years Later

My hand was trapped tightly in Trick's palm and my breathing was ragged and out of control. Adrenaline was snaking through me, causing me to tremble with nerves. He lifted my fingers to his lips and kissed my wedding band softly. "Relax Tink. We got this."

I took a deep breath as he pushed the door open and pulled me tightly into his side. Ashley looked up at us from the bed, exhaustion written all over her face.

"Hey guys. Are you ready to see them?" She smiled and my heart filled with love for this woman who had given me so much.

I nodded eagerly and Trick matched me step for step as we made our way over to the side of the bed. In two matching cribs were two tiny bundled babies. Our babies. One boy, one girl. The little girl freed her hand from the swaddling and her fist reached out in front of her. My skin hummed to make contact with her but I was reluctant to move, too afraid that this was all a dream.

Ashley spoke first. "It's okay Beth. You can hold them, they're yours."

Trick nudged me softly, as eager as I was. I trembled as I picked her up, she was so tiny in my arms. Her eyes opened just a fraction and I saw the beautiful grey of Trick's looking back at me. "She's so beautiful."

Trick touched my shoulder lightly with his and I saw he was holding the little boy in his own arms, the baby utterly dwarfed by the huge size of his father. Father. That word sounded so perfect for him. "We should think of names now Tink."

He'd been pushing me for names for months. In the same way he'd encouraged me to decorate the nursery and buy baby clothes. Except I hadn't been able to do any of that. Despite Ashley carrying the product of my eggs and Trick's sperm melded together in a petri dish, I didn't want to take anything for granted. I'd read so many horror stories about things going wrong with surrogates and this just felt too epic to pin my hopes on. My eyes flicked to Ashley. "Not yet."

Ashley smiled knowingly. We'd chosen her because she'd been a surrogate before and I'd woken up screaming with nightmares of women running off with my babies. I'd insisted she be vetted repeatedly and Trick had patiently entertained my every fantasy with a stoic nod of agreement. "I think you're probably looking for these?" She held out some papers and I stepped towards her, cradling the baby girl protectively.

It was the paperwork to assign us as the legal parents. We couldn't file it until after Ashley had registered the births but somehow seeing it there in front of me made things a little easier to bear. Ashley was still their mother and she could take them away from me at any moment. The thought made me shiver and I held the little girl slightly tighter.

Trick broke the silence. "Ashley. Thank you." His face was as full of love as his heart. He turned to me.

"Tink, stop panicking. We got this babe." His lips touched mine briefly. "You wanna swap?"

I nodded and we did an awkward handover, both of us terrified to drop one. The little boy in my arms had dark brown eyes. "Ben." I said it softly.

"What's that babe?" Trick manoeuvred himself around so he was in front of me.

"Ben. He looks like Ben. I think that should be his name."

Trick grinned. "Yeah. I like that. What about this little beauty?"

I looked at her again and knew with absolute certainty what she should be called. "Lisa."

Trick's eyebrows rose. "Like your mum?"

I nodded. "Yeah. I think she would have liked that." He agreed and kissed me softly, encouraging me to sit down.

My life had not been easy up until this point. Loss and heart break were littered around my timeline like a horror movie. But here, with my husband and these two perfect little babies, I suddenly felt a true sense of peace inside me. This was the start of a new chapter and this time I got to write the lines. And every single one of them would be filled with love and happiness.

End

Trick's Playlist

Support your artists - download legally!

Counting Stars – Onerepublic

Another Love – Tom O'Dell

Wake Me Up – Avicii

This Ruined Heart – The Clarendons

You Can Do Better Than Me – Death Cab for Cutie

A Reflection of Anguish on a Face so Innocent – Autumn to Ashes

A Sadness Runs Through Him – The Hoosiers

The Greatest Fall of All Time – Matchbook Romance

Little Talks – Of Monsters and men

Politico – Penfold Gate

Call it a Day – The Raconteurs

Stand Inside Your Love – The Smashing Pumpkins

My Own Worst Enemy

What Difference Does it Make? – The Smiths

Take Me Back – Story of the Year

Unquestioned Answers – Thrice

Maybe Memories – The Used

Coming Soon!

Five Times

Ben Lewis can't have a relationship. He has a darkness inside him that would taint anyone he was with. He knows it wouldn’t be fair to anyone else to have to suffer through his demons. Until he finally sees Frankie and realises he wants to finally be able to breathe freely again.

Frankie had made a promise and she intends to keep it. No sex until date number six. She's been fantasising about that date being with Ben Lewis for as long as she's known him but he's never seen her that way. Until now.

You can't move forward until you let go of the past.

My Own Worst Enemy

The Replacement

Jackson Fisher - lead singer for indie rock band Wounded Heart has just watched his brother Taylor die. The last thing he wants to consider is replacing Taylor with a new guitarist but the record company have other ideas. When Liam North auditions, Jackson can't help but be distracted by the beautiful and mysterious woman at his side.

Lex North is everything Jackson needs to pull him from his deep depression. She's sexy, sweet, determined and willing to follow Jackson down the rabbit hole. But Lex has a secret that will turn Jackson's world upside down forever...

The Replacement is book one in the Wounded Heart series.

Emma L Smith

Undeniable

Released December 2013

Also available in print from all good retailers

Sometimes in life you're given an opportunity to take a road that the heart cannot deny.

Kate feels like her life is going nowhere. She might love her job but her love life is circling the drain. Her marriage is falling apart and she's not even sure if she wants to save it anymore. Her new boss is egotistical and annoying and frustratingly sexy. She knows she should be fighting for her marriage but she finds his pull undeniable.

My Own Worst Enemy

Cole is feeling the pressure. His father has expectations that he feels he has to live up to. Until Kate is thrust into his life and he has to make a decision to fight for the woman he loves or to give in to his father's demands and risk losing everything.

Acknowledgements

I couldn't have written a single line if it weren't for the support of my husband. He may joke that he's not in any of my books but the truth is that I would never have been inspired if it weren't for the love he shows me every single day. Even on the days when he's reading over my shoulder in a comedy voice.

Sami Smith - I love you chick. You read all of my crap, no matter how bad the first draft is and I love you for it!

All my beta readers - I won't name you in case I accidentally miss someone, but know that without you, this book would probably have ended up in the bin.

Helen Williams at All Booked Out - the first blogger to take a chance on a poor self-pubber and give it a go. I don't even have words for my gratitude and I'm a writer!

My Own Worst Enemy

Anne - you should be the most famous person in the world. Your talent is limitless, thank you for sharing.

To everyone who's ever taken a chance on reading my books, even if you didn't like them - THANK YOU!